A RITUAL OF DEATH

"Let us begin," he said. "Let us get this foolishness over with. You will die tonight. . . Prepare yourself for that. You are but one man and I am the Japanese people."

He bowed once again. I bowed in return.

And then he moved out eagerly, the knife held close to his body, ready to dart and kill, like the streaking head of a deadly serpent.

From The Nick Carter Killmaster Series

NICK CARTER IS IT!

"Nick Carter out-Bonds James Bond."
>
> —*Buffalo Evening News*

"Nick Carter is America's #1 espionage agent."
>
> —*Variety*

"Nick Carter is razor-sharp suspense."
>
> —*King Features*

"Nick Carter is extraordinarily big."
>
> —*Bestsellers*

"Nick Carter has attracted an army of addicted readers . . . the books are fast, have plenty of action and just the right degree of sex . . . Nick Carter is the American James Bond, suave, sophisticated, a killer with both the ladies and the enemy."
>
> —*The New York Times*

NC-A

Dedicated to The Men of the Secret Services of
the United States of America

A Killmaster Spy Chiller

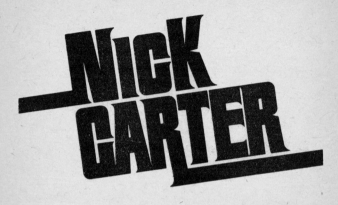

NICK CARTER

DEADLY DOUBLES

CHARTER
NEW YORK

A DIVISION OF CHARTER COMMUNICATIONS INC.
A GROSSET & DUNLAP COMPANY

DEADLY DOUBLES

Charter Books
A Division of Charter Communications, Inc.
A Grosset & Dunlap Company
360 Park Avenue South
New York, New York 10010

Chapter 1

Some people never learn.

Gunther Roessler was one of them.

Seen at a distance, from my vantage point at the edge of the Javanese jungle, he still looked lean and trim. Lit by the morning sun beginning to sear away the fetid mists, he stood on the verandah of the low, sprawling yellow clapboard building that served as his home and the headquarters of his innocuously named Eastern Island Tapioca Company. Carefully brushed, his hair was still trimmed short in the military style, and if some of the blond had begun to fade from those perfect Aryan locks, it was difficult to see where. Even in the moist heat, his shirt—and the trousers tucked into the tops of his high, gleaming jackboots—held their knife-edge creases as though by an act of his Prussian will.

Thirty years had passed, and Gunther Roessler hadn't changed a bit. He still looked just as he had in the days when they called him the Boy Butcher of Belsen.

You can take the boy out of the SS, I thought, but you can't take the SS out of the boy.

1

His left hand gripped a quirt, and watching him through my binoculars, I could see him slapping the leather impatiently across his right palm. The old dueling scar running diagonally from just above the outer corner of his left eye to the base of his left nostril twitched slightly. Somewhere in the compound a whistle blew, and workers began scurrying to assemble outside the headquarters.

I glanced at my watch: 5:30 A.M.

In the compound below, Gunther Roessler snapped the end of the quirt into his palm again.

Curb your impatience, Gunther, I thought. *This is the last day of your life.*

I let the binoculars fall away from my eyes. The workers were forming ranks. The rhythm of the quirt slapping peevishly into Roessler's palm slowed. I was conscious of the jungle damp, the smell of rot, the rays of the morning sun slanting against the back of my neck, a bead of sweat cutting a trail across the terrain of my ribs. If I waited long enough, I knew, bold insects, small animals, birds, and perhaps a snake would wend their way toward me, seeking to examine this large, warm object that lay so still at their jungle's edge— hoping to transform it into food. It was not a pleasant place to be. It was not a safe place to remain for long.

Except for someone like Gunther Roessler.

He had lasted thirty years in the jungle—thirty years among the species who preyed on the weak and defenseless.

He might have lasted another thirty had he not given way to his old sickness.

I thought back to the contents of the dossier that had been given to me in Washington. In my mind's eye, I could see again the cover, with my name and designation on it: NICK CARTER, AXE KILLMASTER, N3.

As though in a film, I saw my hand reaching again to open the cover, to make my acquaintance for the first time with Gunther Roessler, whose scarred teenage face stared out from a faded enlargement of the Boy Butcher as he had looked in his black SS uniform.

Gunther Roessler, the dossier said, had been eighteen years old when the war ended in Europe. But on May 8, 1945, VE Day, he was already in Switzerland, living inconspicuously on the first of his withdrawals from a numbered bank account in Zurich. His passport and identity papers—Swiss documents, of course— were impeccable, the work of a seventy-four-year-old master artisan named Avram Axelrod.

Roessler had taken the old man aside one day at Belsen after learning of his talents. He had promised him an extra ration of food; he had promised him the best of equipment. And he had promised to spare his life.

The old man looked at him skeptically.

The young man smiled his most disarming smile.

"Don't worry," Gunther said.

The old man labored slowly and painstakingly, certain that sloppy work would earn him death. He prolonged the task, in the hope of rescue, gambling that a fine job would, indeed, convince the young Nazi to spare his life.

One winter day in the last months of the war, he finished. Roessler examined the work in the harsh glare of the gooseneck lamp on the old man's work table.

"Good," he murmured, "very good."

Avram Axelrod looked up at him apprehensively.

3

Roessler smiled down on him—an open, boyish smile, marred only by the puckering of the scar that violated his face.

He chuckled disarmingly. "I know what you are thinking, old man," he said. "You are thinking that now that I have no further need of you, I am going to kill you."

Gunther's black gloved hand reached out and patted the old man's cheek. "Don't worry, father," Gunther said. "I have not forgotten my promise. You may go. Your troubles are over. Your future is assured."

Avram Axelrod, who had been trembling, relaxed visibly. Tears trickled down his cheeks. He rose with the slowness of age from his chair, bobbing his head in gratitude toward the black-uniformed Nazi.

As he turned to go through the door, Roessler shot him once in the spine. He died instantly.

By the count of Allied intelligence, whose files were the original source of the story of Avram Axelrod, as related by fellow inmates who witnessed his death, Gunther Roessler personally took the lives of 238 inmates of the Belsen concentration camp. Few were dispatched so quickly.

The majority were subjected to torture, including the removal by hammer of their gold dental inlays, which, when melted down and reshaped more attractively, formed the foundation of Roessler's Zurich bank account.

The 238 deaths were, of course, only a small portion of the total number of lives snuffed out at Belsen under young Roessler's personal supervision.

His superiors considered him quite effective in removing "surplus humanity." If ever a man and his work were ideally mated, it was Gunther Roessler and killing the weak and defenseless.

In the months following the end of the war, intelligence personnel from four Allied nations attempted to pick up his trail. They traced it as far as Lisbon, where it vanished. There was some indication that he had taken up residence in Buenos Aires under the name Guttman. But the two British intelligence officers who made the journey to Argentina late in 1945 returned empty-handed.

According to the AXE dossier, the truth was that by early 1946 Gunther Roessler was quite openly operating the Eastern Island Tapioca Company in what is now Indonesia. True, he concealed his Nazi past, representing himself to be Swiss. But he made no effort to change his name. The name *Roessler*, it happens, is not unknown in the Far East. No history of Japan, for example, is complete without mention of Herman Roessler, a more than influential German adviser of the Japanese Foreign Office in the days of the emperor Meiji, late in the nineteenth century.

Gunther Roessler might have lived out his life without further notice had he concentrated on growing tapioca. But as I said, some people never learn and Gunther Roessler was one of them. He had decided to return to his favorite pursuit: mass death.

It was Nick Carter's job to stop him.

As I lay there at the edge of the jungle, I could see what he had planned. His compound was a re-creation of one of the old World War II concentration camps-- the same low barracks, the death houses, the crematoria. I could not see the burial pits. Perhaps they had not yet been dug.

In my mind's eye, I could see it all happening again. Emaciated figures, gathered up by Roessler for a fee from countries beset by overpopulation, shambling blank-eyed into the gas chambers and the ovens. The old, the women, the children—long lines stretching as far as the eye could see.

Despite the heat, a chill snaked along my spine. I shook my head to clear away the hideous pictures. In my business, reverie is a dangerous pastime.

I was reminded of that fact by a piece of blued steel. It was the barrel of a Colt .357 Python. And it was poking into the base of my skull.

Chapter 2

I did not understand the voice that spoke to me, but its meaning, accompanied by a slight slap of the pistol barrel, was unmistakable: "Roll over."

On my back, I found myself staring up at a strange creature—short, bandy-legged, possessed of a sallow, pitted face with glowing eyes that stared down at me from under a shallow brow surmounted by a wild thatch of pitch-black hair.

He bared his yellow teeth in a snarl and motioned me to my feet with his empty hand. He wore nothing besides a torn khaki shirt and a cloth knotted around his loins. He motioned me toward the compound. At the same time, he emitted a high-pitched whistle.

I saw Gunther Roessler look up and nod. He waved imperiously to his assembled workers, and they trotted off to their tasks, vanishing in a matter of seconds.

A few minutes later, we were standing before him on the porch of his headquarters. He smiled at the creature.

"What's the meaning of this?" I shouted.

Roessler smiled with cynical tolerance.

"I believe that is my question, not yours," he said. "You are trespassing on my property." My binoculars dangled by a strap from his fingers. "And judging by these, you have been spying on me. I will give you exactly one minute to explain yourself. At the end of that time, if I am not satisfied, I will turn you over to Sulak, here. At best, he will kill you with the pistol. It is a new toy I have given him, and he is eager to use it. At worst, he will stake you out in the jungle after making your body attractive to its inhabitants with spices, blood, and a bit of intestine—the latter two being yours, of course."

Sulak stepped up behind me and patted me down. He did not find Hugo, my stiletto, or Wilhelmina, my Luger. I had left them in the five-speed Toyota Celica, waiting for me a mile from where I had taken up my position at the edge of the jungle. As for Pierre, the little gas bomb I wore like a third testicle, Sulak's imagination did not permit him to find it.

"You see," I told Roessler, "I am unarmed."

Roessler smiled. "Yes," he said. "We have your pistol and your knife inside. Your arrival did not go unnoticed. Sulak needs very little sleep, and he has the instincts of an animal. He sensed something amiss early this morning. Perhaps he smelled you. There is very little we know about Sulak. Open your mouth, Sulak!"

Sulak opened his mouth. It was not a pretty sight.

"Sulak has no tongue," Roessler said. "He was like that when I found him out here when I first arrived. So he could not tell me what became of his parents. In any event, he has remained with me ever since, a most loyal and trustworthy servant."

Sulak's eyes glittered.

8

"If I tell him to kill you," Roessler said, "he will kill you. And he will not hesitate."

I gestured toward Sulak, who still pointed the Colt at me with unwavering concentration.

"I believe I can explain everything to your satisfaction, Mr. Roessler," I said. "If you will encourage Sulak here to do nothing hasty, I believe I can begin to convince you that my presence here is to our mutual benefit."

"Really?" Roessler said. "I find that hard to believe, but I am willing to hear you out. Here in the jungle, a good story is always welcome. And Sulak, though loyal, is scarcely garrulous. Come inside."

Sulak accompanied us into the headquarters. There was nothing lavish about the large rooms. The floors were bare. Simple rattan furniture was the sole adornment. Screened rattan windows gaped wide in invitation to any breeze that might find its way under the overhanging roof that protected the rooms as well as possible from the sun's glare.

"Have a seat," Roessler said. "It is a bit too early to offer you a drink, but I believe we can spare a cup of coffee for you before whatever is to happen, happens."

He clapped his hands.

A girl, no more than twelve or thirteen, padded out on bare feet almost before the sound had faded. She bore a single cup of coffee on a wooden tray. Sulak's eyes followed her as she returned to the kitchen.

I took a sip of the coffee.

"All right!" Roessler's voice was sharp now. "Enough of the amenities. Who are you, and why have you been spying on me?"

"With your permission—and with Sulak's indulgence," I said, "I would like to reach into my trousers pocket and take out my wallet."

"Please do," Roessler said. "But slowly. It would be dangerous to allow Sulak to think for a moment that you meant me any harm."

"Understood," I said. In a moment, I was holding a little business card. "I am here on business, Mr. Roessler," I said.

He raised an eyebrow.

"I doubt that you are engaged in any business that might interest me," he said.

"I'm not so sure of that," I said.

"Really?" he said. "Just what business are you engaged in?"

I tried to restrain myself from smiling with the irony of it. "Extermination," I said. I handed him the card. "Nicholas Carter," it said. "Far Eastern Manager. General Enterprises. New York. New Delhi. Hong Kong. Tokyo."

Roessler read it, turned it over, and, finding its back blank, scaled it back at me. "It tells me nothing," he said.

"It would hardly benefit either of us to be more specific in print," I said.

"Come to the point. I'm growing weary of this," Roessler said.

Sulak thumbed back the hammer of the Python. I tried not to think what that .357 bullet would feel like. He was about seven feet away. At fifteen feet, I knew, the bullet would penetrate twelve inches of pine board.

Roessler was right. It was time to come to the point.

"My firm is interested in contracting with you in your new enterprise."

Roessler's eyes widened.

"That's right," I said. "We understand you are about to establish a service for those who are interested in reducing the population glut."

"But how did you know?"

"Mr. Roessler, a few months ago, you placed some orders for certain lethal gasses in large quantities through a concern in New Delhi. That concern was not part of General Enterprises, but nevertheless, it is difficult to conceal word of such an order from making the rounds. Even you will concede that it was somewhat unusual."

"Quite so," Roessler said.

"It did not take long for my concern to guess why it was being ordered, and—being an enterprising corporation—General Enterprises began ever-so-discreetly to test the market, so to speak."

"And?" Roessler said.

"The results were remarkable."

Roessler smiled. "I could have told you as much," he said. "I may be isolated here in a backward outpost where news penetrates slowly, if at all, but I could have told you as much. Did you waste much money on your market studies, Mr. Carter?"

He was positively bubbling with self-esteem. A little flattery wouldn't hurt, I decided. "I must compliment you, Mr. Roessler," I said. "For one so isolated to have sensed that the time was ripe for such a business is nothing short of a stroke of genius."

Roessler beamed. It was like opening the floodgates.

"You are too generous," he said. "Study the world only superficially, and what do you see? Shortages of food everywhere. Soaring energy costs. The prospect of continuing depletion of the earth's irreplaceable natural resources."

I nodded at him blithely.

"Fools talk about conservation," he said, "about mining the sea for food and minerals, about developing synthetic fuels and alternate energy sources. Such plans solve nothing. The trouble with the world is very simple. Too many people."

I nodded encouragement.

"This planet cannot support its population," Roessler went on. "Given the working of natural laws, the weak would die, and nature would generously support those who remain. But no! The natural laws are not permitted to work. Efforts are made in the name of civilization to preserve the weak, the sickly, the unfit. Idiocy!"

His face was more animated than at any time since I had laid eyes on him. A faint flush suffused his pale skin as he continued. "Some people die, of course, but at an unnaturally slow rate." He shook his head despairingly. "Too slowly. Too slowly. The rate must be accelerated. And that," he added with a smile of self-satisfaction, "accounts for the establishment of my new venture."

He was really something to see. Not a trace of conscience. Not a glimmering of awareness of the colossal evil he sought to perpetrate again. No glimmer of civilizing influence. No respect for humanity. The perfect barbarian; the perfect relic of the Third Reich;

preserved like a fossil in a tar pit; with all its repugnant characteristics still intact, with no lessons learned, with no knowledge that those who cannot learn from history are doomed to repeat it.

"The morality of it," I said. "Doesn't it bother you?"

For the first time Roessler laughed. He laughed until he coughed and tears trickled from the corners of his eyes. Even Sulak—dim, deadly Sulak—was caught up in the merriment. From his tongueless mouth issued a high-pitched whinny.

"Wonderful, wonderful!" Roessler said. "You must be an American, Mr. Carter. I have heard Americans have a wonderful sense of humor. But in the event you are serious, I must tell you that what I propose to do is highly moral. To exterminate the unfit and unproductive is to ensure the greater good and the survival of the world. And that, I suggest to you, is a most decidedly moral position."

He waved his hand airily.

"Enough of such talk," he said. "We are both businessmen, Mr. Carter. What does morality matter to us, eh? I have something to sell. You wish to buy. We do business."

"Yes," I said. "The business of death. Let's get on with it."

"In a moment, my friend," Roessler said. "I think you deserve a drink, despite what I said before about the earliness of the hour." He clapped three times.

The girl reappeared and set down a tray with a bottle and two glasses.

Sulak eyed her hungrily.

Roessler smiled at him indulgently. "Sulak," he said. "You have done a good morning's work. You wish the girl? Take her."

No sooner had the words left his mouth, than Sulak's ape-like arm had reached out and seized the girl, ripping the sackcloth from her thin body.

She stood impassive, resigned, not even attempting to cover herself with her arms.

Sulak laid down his pistol and wriggled out of his shirt and breechclout. Roessler appeared to take all this as nothing extraordinary. He lifted the bottle from the tray, poured the liquor into glasses, and beckoned me to take a seat.

Sulak grasped the girl by her long black tresses, pulling her head back until her knees buckled and she slid to the bare wooden floor. With an animal cry, he hurled himself upon her.

The girl screamed and then lay silent while Sulak ground himself violently against her thin loins.

I tossed my drink down my throat. Roessler watched, half-smiling between sips of his liquor.

"Amusing, no?" he said.

I pretended not to hear him.

"Diversion is so rare out here," he said.

Glistening with sweat, Sulak gave a last convulsive shudder, accompanied by an eerie cry of release, and lay still atop his conquest. After a moment he rolled away from her and began to dress. The girl remained motionless on the floor, a thin rill of diluted blood between her thighs.

"Get rid of her," Roessler said.

Sulak dragged her outside.

"Now," he said. "Now business."

"Are your facilities ready for operation?" I asked.

"Yes," he said. "We can dispose of ten thousand a day. No doubt you have noticed that we are situated not far from a deep-water cove. They can be brought in by ship, with no one the wiser. The gas chambers are in readiness. The crematoria are in readiness. The burial pits, not yet. But it is only a matter of a few hours' work once the first shipments arrive. Forgive me, Mr. Carter, but where do you propose to bring in your shipments from?"

I smiled enigmatically.

"I understand," he said. "It is premature of me to ask. But after all the planning that has gone into this enterprise, you can forgive my curiosity. Which of the world's overpopulated sites is to be the source of my gain? India? Japan?" He smiled. "Perhaps even the United States, where, I understand, there are too many of the elderly."

I smiled again.

He shrugged. "Well, time will tell. I shall restrain my impatience."

Sulak reentered the room.

"What I should like now," I said, "is to inspect the gas chambers."

"Most assuredly," Roessler said. "A little more schnapps before we go?"

"Yes, I think so," I said.

He refilled our glasses.

"Prosit!" he shouted, and tossed down his drink.

I raised my glass. "To your future," I said. I looked squarely into his pale blue eyes and swallowed my drink.

"Come, my friend," he said.

"One moment," I said. "Before we go, might I use your lavatory?"

"By all means."

Inside, I removed Pierre, the little gas bomb, from its hiding place and stowed it within easy reach in my jacket pocket. With it went the little clip that doubled as a breather.

I flushed the toilet and spat into the swirling water. "To your future, Gunther," I said softly.

The gas chamber they took me to was one of five, neatly concealed by the jungle foliage. It resembled an old army barracks, with its yellow boarding and sloping green roof.

"Come inside." Roessler beckoned.

I hesitated.

He laughed. "Do not worry, my friend. Sulak and I will be with you."

I pretended to manage a wan smile. "Well," I said, "I hear there's safety in numbers."

I pushed past them and walked inside. Sulak closed the door behind us. We were in a long, empty room with a shiny green linoleum floor.

"It looks so innocent," I said.

"That is the beauty of it," Roessler said. "Who is to suspect? Yet the room is air-tight. Even now, there is only enough air to last us for a few minutes. And look, up there." He gestured toward the ceiling fans. "They look so harmless. But they are not. I pull a switch outside, and in minutes every living thing in here has been gassed to death. If you wish, we can do it while they are asleep. I have some cots available. We can arrange for it to look like a dormitory. We also have the gas chambers that resemble communal showers. Or we can simply herd them in here *en masse*. Any way you like. What is it you say? Take your choice, quality or quantity.''

"Quite remarkable," I said. "And you say it's all air-tight.''

"Absolutely," Roessler said. "Those windows are sealed. So is the door. Air-tight rubber edging.''

He glanced at his watch. "A minute or two more and we shall begin to grow uncomfortable unless we leave.''

"I just can't believe it," I said, shaking my head. "You say another minute and the air will be gone?''

"Indeed," he said.

"That's wonderful!" I shouted. "I took a deep draught of the remaining air, clapped the breather to my nose, and tossed Pierre at Sulak's feet.

He reacted quickly, bending down to reach the little ball splitting its deadly jet of poison gas.

I brought my foot into his face, spattering his nose in a streak of bloody gristle across his cheekbones. He fell to the floor, and the Python flipped out of his breech-clout. He would have the pleasure of dying unconscious.

Coughing, Roessler dived for the pistol. I reached it first, crunching his hand under my heel.

"You bastard!" he said.

"An angel, compared to you.''

A paroxysm shook his body. His face began to blue. He rolled over on his back.

"Who sent you?" he said. Vomit welled up out of his throat.

I waited until he finished gagging. "AXE," I said.

His eyes rolled upward. His mind drifted into the past, back, back to the last winter of the war. "AXE," he gasped. "Axelrod. Avram Axelrod. Gott in himmel!"

And then he twitched and lay dead.

Roessler's workers—or were they slaves?—showed no inclination to avenge their master's death. Judging by his treatment of the girl sacrificed to Sulak's amusement, he was probably not very popular.

So I was able to go about the remainder of my business at a leisurely pace. I went back to the headquarters first and retrieved Hugo and Wilhelmina. Then I treated myself to a look through Roessler's files. For the most part, it was an excursion through the thickets of business correspondence. He dealt mostly with firms in Japan and India. Dull stuff.

In the back of his desk drawer I found a cigarette lighter emblazoned with a black swastika and the rising red sun of Japan, neatly enameled into the gleaming silver. Beneath the two, engraved hands clasped. Souvenir of the Axis, I supposed.

When I had satisfied myself about his files, I returned to my car and took out the plastique that had escaped Sulak's uneducated scrutiny.

By 9:30 A.M. I had blown Gunther Roessler's evil dream into rubble.

Not a bad morning's work, I told myself as I pointed the car back toward Jakarta.

Mission accomplished.

Or so I thought.

Chapter 3

Pan Am flight 812 leaves Djakarta's Kamajoran Airport at 9:25 P.M. Mondays. It is the best of their flights to the United States—Djakarta, Sydney, Honolulu, Los Angeles, arriving at 5:20 P.M. Wednesday.

I took my time driving back from the Far Eastern Tapioca plantation. The roads were none too good anyway. Darkness was falling by the time I approached the outskirts of Djakarta.

In the distance, a bright glow lit the sky. As I drew closer, I could see the cause—an enormous blaze sending huge tongues of flame licking hungrily at the night sky. A warehouse burning, I thought.

Beside me as I drove, I could see the tiny woven bamboo huts of the squatters who had trudged in toward the capital from the impoverished villages of West Java, hoping for work. Outside one of them, an emaciated woman clothed in a filthy rag held a frail-looking child to her withered breast. Flies buzzed about the child's nostrils. The stench of filth and decay rose from the encampment.

In a moment, it was behind me. Ahead, the glow of the sky grew brighter, but beside the road, the vista was more pleasant. Lavish suburban homes lined the way.

And then I was in the city, weaving my way through narrow streets. Suddenly, ahead of me, a mob surged around the corner—ten abreast—with no end in sight, shrieking with fury, brandishing torches, clubs, steel bars.

They were out for blood—and the blood was about to be mine. I stood on the brakes when they were 150 feet away and slammed the synchromesh transmission into reverse. As my eyes flicked toward the rear-view mirror, I could see I was too late. Another section of the rioting mob had rounded the corner behind me, torches flaring, throats shrieking hatred at the flame-bloodied night sky.

I looked ahead again. A piece of stone crashed against the windshield, turning it into a impenetrable web of fractured glass. Another rock smashed against the rear window.

Now they were closer. Clubs and bars rained down against the fenders in a grotesque symphony of destruction. Through the side windows, howling, angry faces sang some incomprehensible opera of loathing. I slid Hugo into my hand. A knife would be better for the close work.

A side window cracked. Again a club smashed against it. The mob swarmed too closely about the little car for me to open the door. A man clutching a flaming brand peered into the one remaining whole window. He grinned at me crazily out of a toothless mouth. He pointed to his torch and then gestured unmistakably toward the gas tank.

His meaning was all too clear. He was going to plunge that torch into the gasoline. And when he did, I would die a hideous death on a funeral pyre of red-hot steel and melting rubber.

Outside the incredible racket continued—the howling of angry voices, the ceaseless hammering of clubs on cars, the continuous battering at the now opaque windows. And then the window nearest me exploded in a spray of finely powdered glass. A hand reached in and yanked open the door. Rough hands were pulling me from the car. The mob was engulfing me. A geyser of flame shot up from the Toyota. Off-balance, I felt myself being dragged backwards, stumbling, tripping, out of control in a maelstrom of violence. Then pain. Then darkness.

When I awoke, my aching head was resting on a pile of tattered sacking. An old man squatted beside me. When he saw my eyes flicker, he edged forward and pressed a damp cloth against my brow.

I sat up. There was a lump on my skull, and a bit of matted blood, but things could have been worse. I was surprised to discover Hugo beside me.

"The people wish you to know they are sorry," the old man said. "It was not you they were after. Only the car."

I must have looked as puzzled as I was.

"The car," he said. "It is Japanese. The people are angry at the Japanese. They come here. They make much money in business. Yet our people are without work. They hunt in the streets for discarded cigarettes and then sell them for a few rupiahs a day. Eleven million of my people have no work. Eighteen million have less than enough work. Perhaps you have seen the squatters' villages.''

I nodded.

"And perhaps you have seen the wealthy suburbs, and the skyscrapers and the big cars that roll along the Jalan M. H. Thamrin.''

I nodded again. I had seen the big cars on the main drag.

"Then you know why my people are angry,'' the old man said.

Once more I nodded.

"I hope, therefore, you will forgive them.''

I rubbed the knob on my head. "No harm done,'' I told him.

"Good,'' the old man said. "I believe we have interrupted your journey; so permit us to make amends.''

A few minutes later, one of the three-wheeled *becaks* was waiting outside.

"Where do you wish to go, master?'' a young man said.

"To the airport.''

"Pedal him in safety, Jusuf,'' the old man said.

An hour later, I was watching my fellow passengers board flight 812. It was what I would call the usual crossroads-of-the-world assortment when it came to the businessmen types—a few Americans, including my-self, a handful of Germans, a half dozen Swiss, perhaps a score of Japanese, and a lone Arab.

"You have your passport?" the pert blonde stewardess was saying.

"Yiss, yiss," answered the Japanese.

The girl was busy making little checks against a flight manifest.

"Mr. Suzuki? Mr. Fukunaka? Mr. Higuchi?"

"Yiss. Yiss. Yiss."

The Germans. "Mr. Heinsdorf? Mr. Schmidt?"

"Jah. Jah."

"Mr. Carter?"

"Yes," I said.

"Going all the way?" she asked.

"All the way," I said.

I was busy settling into my seat when she checked off the last of the names, the Arab.

"Mr. Jabal-Zahab?"

"Yes," I heard him say.

I made myself comfortable in a bulkhead seat, where I would have room to stretch my legs on the long flight. The plane was uncrowded, and no one sat beside me. Behind me, I could hear the Japanese giggling and clicking the shutters of their cameras. Then came the high whine of engines and the streaking run down the tarmac past the Bouraq and Guruda Indonesian Airways planes and into the night sky. Down below I could see the fierce glow of the fires set by the rioters. There was a burst of excited chatter from the Japanese. Across the way and a few rows behind, two of them pressed the lenses of their cameras to the windows and clicked away at the inferno below.

When the seat-belt sign was turned off, I rose and went for a stroll toward the rear of the plane. Mister

Jabal-Zahab was busily draping his head in a blanket taken from an overhead rack, settling in for the night like a desert bedouin. When I strolled back, he was completely covered, his snores competing faintly with the noise of the jet engines outside.

When I sat down again, it was not long before the pert blonde stewardess was standing beside me.

"Is there something I can do for you?" she said.

"Now or later?" I asked.

She smiled; then leaned over me as though to adjust my seat. Her full breasts crushed themselves against my arm.

"Both, perhaps," she said.

"I'll have something to drink now," I said. "Some Scotch on the rocks."

"Scotch on the rocks," she said. "And later, dinner and the movie and dessert?"

"Sounds inviting," I said. "But shouldn't it be dinner and dessert and the movie?"

She smiled enigmatically and spun rapidly, to head for the galley. The neat pirouette swirled her skirt, directing my eyes to her spectacular legs.

Dinner was the usual rot dished up by airlines, a miracle of packaging and a debacle of cuisine. A soggy piece of sponge cake topped with a wrinkled cherry stared up at me from the dessert compartment. I left it uneaten.

"Didn't like your dessert?" the stewardess asked when she came to remove the tray. Her blue eyes twinkled.

"No," I said.

"Oh, my," she said. "The commissary chefs will be

so disappointed. They try so hard. What was it that turned you off? Was it the cherry?"

She didn't wait for an answer. "Yes, it must have been the cherry. Sometimes it's better without the cherry. Well, let me say I'm sorry. If you've got a tooth for sweets, maybe we can find you something to sink it into later on tonight." She patted my thigh. "We'll see. I'll be clearing things away now, but I'll stop by later and see if there's anything special you want."

She was back in ten minutes, leaning over again. "I'm going to set things up for the movie now," she said. "It's not a very good movie—one of those secret-agent things. I'd suggest you just lean back and relax and forget all about it."

The interior of the plane went dark. On the screen there was a surge of running figures, followed by flashes of gunfire and spurts of blood. I did not bother with the earphones. I closed my eyes. I had almost drifted into sleep, when I became conscious of her beside me.

She was standing, her body stretched taut as she reached to the rack above my seat. Her full breasts thrust against the thin fabric of her blouse. I closed my eyes again. She draped the thin blanket over me and slid in beside me, lifting the armrest out of the way.

In a moment her searching hand found my crotch. Her lips coursed gently against my ear, and her warm breath stirred delicate nerves.

"I'm serving dessert now," she said. "Something homemade and just for you."

Her fingers slid into my trousers, and I pulled her toward me.

Up on the screen, someone was running down a long corridor while bullets chipped pieces out of the wall beside him.

I crushed my lips against hers and she met my kiss with undisguised eagerness.

I slid my hand under her skirt, along the silken flesh of her bare thighs, to the warm pool of moistness that was an invitation beyond words.

"Oh!" she said. "Oh, yes!"

In a moment, she had swiveled herself across my loins, thrusting herself against me in a thirsty paroxysm of ecstasy.

"Yes," she said. "Yes and yes again!"

I surged up to meet her in a blending of hungers, sated for each of us in explosive release.

Later, while someone ducked the fingers of probing searchlights outside a barbed-wire compound up on the screen, she nestled in the crook of my arm.

"Did you like dessert?" she said.

"Yes," I said. "Homemade is always the best."

"I'm glad you liked it," she said. "You can have it whenever convenient, all the way to the U.S.A."

It was a nice trip.

It was less eventful, though, for most of the passengers. A few of the Japanese disembarked at Sydney. A few more got on, along with a couple of jolly Australians and a sour-looking Frenchman. At Honolulu, the plane filled up with tourists. Some more of the Japanese got off, and some more got on. Like me, Mr. Jabal-Zahab was going all the way—making the entire journey. Whenever I passed by, he seemed to be huddled under his blanket.

I said goodbye to Polly, the blonde stewardess, during a short but appropriately named layover in Honolulu. When the plane landed in Los Angeles, we only exchanged knowing smiles.

"Goodbye," she said. "Hope you enjoyed your journey."

"Yes, indeed," I said.

I was among the last to leave the plane.

As I paused at the top of the exit ramp, I heard her voice one last time.

"We're here now, Mr. Jabal-Zahab. Time to get off. Mr. Jabal-Zahab? Wake up, sir. Sir? Oh, my God!"

Chapter 4

Beneath Dupont Circle in Washington, in the inner sanctum of the Amalgamated Press and Wire Service—the cover name for AXE—David Hawk sat in his rumpled tweeds, wreathed in the foul blue smoke of his omnipresent cigar.

The dossier on Gunther Roessler lay on the desk before him, and as he spoke he tapped its cover with the nicotine-stained fingers that pincered the sodden stub of his smelly pacifier.

My opinion of his cigars must have shown on my face.

"Be of good cheer, Nicholas," he said. "Relations with Cuba seem capable of taking a turn for the better. A year, perhaps two, and maybe I'll be able to get a good Havana again."

"And maybe not," I said. "I ran into one of their people last year in Tangiers. He says they're not growing the tobacco as well as they used to."

"Is he still alive?" Hawk asked.

"No," I said. "A week or so later someone found him in an alley with a .38 slug through his head."

"That goes to show you," Hawk said.

"Show you what?"

"He couldn't have been so smart."

Sometimes Hawk can be very convoluted indeed. But I suppose it's for the best. He's running AXE, and AXE is a pretty good operation, if I do say so.

Hawk took a last puff on the cigar and ground it into a brass ashtray filled with other mashed stubs. The smell was worse than ever. I began to hope he was right about relations with Cuba. Maybe the guy in Tangiers had been wrong. Maybe a good Havana cigar would do wonders for the aroma of Hawk's office.

Hawk shook his head. "Don't get me distracted with talk of cigars," he said. "I'm not supposed to be down here wasting taxpayers' money talking about cigars."

"Well, I think it's justified," I said. "Look at it this way—it's really a discussion about relations with Cuba, and surely that falls within the area of authorized concern of the man who heads AXE."

Hawk waved his hand disgustedly through the air between us. "Enough blarney," he said. "Where's my goddamn cigar?" He reached into the mess in his ashtray and shuffled the butts around, releasing a new burst of foul odor before realizing that all the cigars in the tray were dead.

One wrinkled, liver-spotted hand darted into the upper-right-hand desk drawer and pulled out a fresh cigar. The other was already waiting with a flaming wooden match, struck on a piece of sandpaper pasted to the side of his swivel chair.

"So Roessler is dead," he said. "I can't say I'm sorry. He had it coming to him for a long time. And if he didn't have it coming to him for what he had already done, he'd have had it coming to him for what he was about to do. We can do without any more death camps."

Hawk pulled on his cigar before continuing. "Sure," he said, "you can argue the earth is overpopulated. But it's not a problem you solve by killing people. I have enough faith in the intelligence of man to believe that there are other solutions besides extermination. I've seen death camps, Nick. And I don't want to see any more."

He poked at the dossier again. "There's something you didn't read in here," he said. "Remember the part where it said that after the war personnel from four of the Allied nations went hunting for Roessler? Well, I was one of them."

David Hawk had just made a pretty long speech, and now I knew why.

"I never gave up hoping that someday we'd get wind of him again. I'll put through some calls tomorrow to some of my old friends overseas. They'll be happy to hear the news. Like me, some of them have long memories and don't mind bearing a grudge in a good cause."

He was in a pretty genial mood, so I thought it was a good time to put in a little request I'd had in mind, but before I could say anything, he was talking on, his teeth nipping the end of his cigar.

"Now, Roessler—you think he was working alone?" Hawk asked.

"No particular evidence to the contrary," I said. "I had time to go through his files and his personal belongings. Nothing out of the ordinary. Correspondence with firms in India and Japan."

"You found his orders for the poison gas?"

"No," I said. "I picked up that part of the story by word of mouth. I told Roessler I had heard about it in New Delhi. The truth was, it was picked up in Tokyo. No indication of where the stuff came from or who handled the order. Probably done through cutouts. But still, there was no indication that Roessler had any partners."

"Hmmph," Hawk said.

"What's that supposed to mean?" I asked.

"Hmmph, that's what," Hawk said, glowering. "Hummmph. Just goddamn hummmph."

Well, that was typical of him. Do the man a favor, wipe out a thirty year old score for him, and he's still not satisfied. I suppose he would have liked a letter somewhere in Roessler's desk that said:

Dear Mr. Hawk:
    This is to assure you that I did everything
    all by myself and have no partners.

                Yours truly,
                Gunther Roessler,
                War Criminal.

Well, life—and death—doesn't work that way. Roessler's desk! What was it about that desk? Ah, yes. "One thing," I said to Hawk.

"What?"

"In Roessler's desk I found a cigarette lighter. Enameled Nazi and Japanese flags on one side; clasped hands underneath. A World War II souvenir, I suppose."

"Really?" said Hawk. "Funny I never saw one."

I didn't like the note of reproach in his voice. It was time for me to change the subject.

"Look," I said, "I'm taking a vacation."

Hawk's heavy eyebrows shot up into the low layer of smoke that floated about just at forehead level.

"You're what?"

"Taking a vacation. There's someone I've got to see."

"There's always someone you've got to see," Hawk snapped. "Damned wonder you've got any energy to spare for government business."

Hawk's not the only one with a temper. I could feel the back of my neck getting a little red.

"Now, look," I said. "This isn't just anyone I'm talking about."

Hawk's cigar had gone out. He put a match to it, peering at me over the glowing stub like a man sighting along the barrel of a snub-nosed pistol.

He sucked in some smoke. "Go on," he said.

"The vacation," I said. "There's a reason I want it now. A week, two weeks, a month or two from now may be too late. The lady's dying."

Hawk's expression softened. "I'm sorry," he said. "All right, Nick, go ahead. Take what you need."

"Thanks," I told him.

"But I still don't like it."

I felt the red creeping up my neck again. Hawk must have sensed my anger. He waved a mollifying hand at me.

"Don't get sore, Nick," he said. "Look at that map up there."

There was a map of the world on the wall behind his chair. It had been there for as long as I could remember. If you looked at it closely, you could see that it was covered with tiny pinholes. They marked the world's trouble spots. In times past, the push pins had been clustered in Berlin, Korea, Cuba, Quemoy and Matsu, along the Sino-Soviet border, in Indonesia. Now the map was bare.

"So?" I said. "What's the trouble?"

"The trouble is," said Hawk, "that there's no trouble. And that's why I don't like your going away."

As I said, Hawk's got a funny way of looking at things. I told him so.

"At least when there's trouble, you know where it is and what to do about it," he said. "It's when you can't see the trouble that it's scary."

"May be there is no trouble," I said.

Hawk made a gesture of contempt. "Don't kid yourself," he said. "There's always trouble. It's only a question of where it's coming from. It used to be easy to spot. People would move troops or start building ships and planes. They'd fire shots and drop bombs. They'd cross borders and seize land. I hate to say it, but in this business those were the good old days. You knew who your enemies were, where they were, and what they were up to. It's different now. Nobody needs to make that kind of war any more. You manipulate the money supply or oil or wheat, you make a few quarts of germs in a secret lab, you steal some plutonium.

"It's not just governments you've got to look out for," he went on. "It's the goddamn freelancers, too. They scare me more than anything, Nick. The goddamn freelancers. The fanatics with an ax to grind and money to spend and a willingness to use terror. We've seen enough of it these last few years. The hijackings, the kidnappings, the random bombings, the massacres. And in the middle of it all, there's always someone innocent. Little kids, helpless women, some guy who just happened to be passing by."

He jerked his thumb over his shoulder toward the map behind him. "So that's what I don't like. I don't like the fact that there aren't any pins in my map."

"Well, cheer up," I said. "If you're right, something is bound to turn up soon."

"That's my only consolation, Nick," he said, sucking again on his cigar. His fingers tapped once more on the Roessler doissier. "Now, tell me," he said. "This Roessler business is all wrapped up, eh?"

I nodded.

"And you did him in with Pierre, your little gas bomb."

"Right again," I said.

"You're sure about that," Hawk said.

"Of course I'm sure."

"You couldn't be mistaken? It wasn't the stiletto or the Luger?"

"What are you driving at?" I said.

"I just want to be sure you're sure. And that particular Pierre you used, it was the only gas bomb you had with you?"

"That's right," I said. "What the hell is this?"

"You haven't been doing a little freelancing yourself, have you?" Hawk said.

"Now what the hell is that supposed to mean?"

"Let me ask the questions for a while," Hawk said. "You flew back to Los Angeles on flight 812—the Pan American flight that leaves Djakarta on Mondays at 9:25 P.M.?"

"That's right."

"Well," Hawk said, "when that flight arrived in Los Angeles yesterday morning, one of the passengers was found dead. A Mr. Jabal-Zahab, late of Abu Dhabi. Seller of oil."

"So?"

"You didn't happen to notice Mr. Jabal-Zahab, did you?"

"As it happens, I did," I said. "Little guy with a round face, heavy beard. Spent most of his time under his blanket. That's what made him conspicuous."

"It also made him a convenient target for his killer."

"What do you mean?"

"You really don't know, do you?" Hawk asked.

"Know what?" I said.

"How he was killed."

"Hell, no," I said.

"Well, I'll tell you," Hawk said. "While Mr. Jabal-Zahab was catching forty winks under that makeshift desert tent of his, someone slipped a little gas bomb in there with him. When the plane landed, the gas—just enough to do in our little friend—had dispersed. An autopsy showed what it was. But of course, that was all too late for Mr. Jabal-Zahab. He was one very dead Arab."

"Okay, but I didn't do it."

"Well, you know you didn't do it, and I believe you didn't do it. But when the investigation of that homicide began and when certain other government agencies did a little checking on the passenger manifest of flight 812, you know damn well whose name attracted a certain amount of attention."

"Well, I guess it's only logical," I said.

"Dammit, Nick, I don't like this. Okay, you didn't do it. But whoever did do it wanted it to look like you did it. The question is: Why?"

Hawk's brow furrowed. He mashed his cigar into the brass tray. "What the hell is this all about?"

"Look," I said, "I'm going on vacation. Remember?"

"I remember," he said.

"So you ponder the heavy questions, okay?"

"Sure," Hawk said.

I got up to go. I was at the door when he spoke again.

"Do you know what Joe Louis once said?" he asked.

"Tell me."

"He said you can run, but you can't hide."

"You could say that about Roessler," I said.

"He isn't the only one."

Chapter 5

Nestled in a tiny vale between the mountains and the sea that sweeps the coast of Wales, the small white cottage stood on a circle of greenward embrace by a stalwart ring of trees.

There, amid the glory of nature, in the wild, clean countryside of her birth, Taffy Evans had come home to die.

I made my way to England by plane, to Wales by train, and to the cottage in an ancient cart, driven by an ancient man who clucked to his ancient horse as it plodded, half-sleeping, up from the seacoast village and into the vale.

He left me at the roadside and touched his forefinger to his threadbare cap by way of thanks for my fare, and as I began to make my way through the trees, I could hear him clucking to the horse as they began to plod back down to the village.

She was waiting in the doorway, her face lit by the sun slanting in golden columns between the scudding clouds, the wind drawing the flaming mane of her hair back from her breathtaking face as though on order from heaven to give the lie to death.

I stood stock still for a moment, while her dark green eyes held me across the distance that separated us. The tension grew.

The wind stirred her hair again, and the sun glistened on her full red lips. She smiled and raised her hand in greeting.

Taffy dying? It wasn't possible. Not this wild, beautiful woman from a wild, beautiful countryside. Not the girl who had run off to London when she was fourteen, danced and sung on the West End stage before she was fifteen, been London's most expensive model before she was sixteen, been courted by royalty of three countries before she was seventeen, caused two duels before she was eighteen, acted—and acted well—in three movies before she was nineteen, married a count before she was twenty, and been widowed before she was twenty-one.

She was smart, she was talented, she was brave, and she was tough. She had saved my life once. And I had saved hers.

"There is an old Chinese belief," she had told me then. "If you save someone's life, you are responsible for him forever."

"Then I guess we are responsible for each other forever," I had said.

"I like that," she said. "Very much."

"I like it too."

And now she was dying, and it was impossible to believe. I stood there staring. And she stood staring back. And then all at once she began to run toward me across the deep green grass, and I was running toward her. And she was in my arms, and her lips were on mine, and the wind wrapped me in the silken mane of her hair, and her body molded itself to mine. My nostrils quickened to the fresh scent of her. My hands and fingers raced hungrily into the familiar curves and crannies of her body, and she moaned with the pleasure of it and bared herself to me and drew me to her, moaning with want until her deep cries and shuddering body signaled her powerful release.

When it was finished, we lay side by side on our backs on the grass, staring up at the graying sky through the circle of trees. She held my hand. Our thighs touched. I felt the heat of her.

"It's true, Nick," she said.

I pretended not to hear or know.

"It's true," she said again.

"What is?" I said.

"I'm dying. You didn't believe it. I could see it in your eyes when you first caught sight of me. I know what you were thinking: *She looks too healthy–she can't be dying.* Sometimes I look at myself in the mirror and think the same thing. But it's true, Nick. I'm dying. It's something with the blood. One of those rare diseases. I've seen half a dozen specialists. They all agree.

"It's just a matter of time, and when it happens, it will be quick. Sometimes I feel sorry for myself. And sometimes I think I'm very lucky. I've lived more than most people, I tell myself. I've packed so much into just a few years. More than most people. Why should I have any regrets? I've seen it all, done it all. 'You're a lucky girl, Taffy,' I tell myself. Lucky, lucky, luck——''

Her voice broke, and sobs burst out of her. I held her in my arms till the heaving of her body subsided. I kissed the salt tears from her eyes.

"Oh, Nick," she said. "I'm sorry. I didn't want you to see me like this. I didn't want to cry. I just wanted you to know it was true, to get used to the fact that there is no hope, to talk about it and get it out of the way, so we could put it behind us and enjoy ourselves for a while, so we wouldn't have to talk about it any more."

"Okay," I said. "We won't."

And we didn't.

We walked together inside the cottage. I got down the bottle of Strathisla whiskey she kept in the cupboard over the sink and poured some into a pair of tumblers and set them down on the rough-hewn kitchen table.

"I drink to you, Miss Taffy Evans," I said. "You are the pride of Welsh womanhood. And were I a marryin' man, I would have you for my bride this very day."

She raised her glass.

"And I drink to you, Mr. Nicholas Carter. You represent all that is good in America. And if I were much of a marryin' woman, I'd accept your proposal."

"Then," I said, "takin' the word for the deed, let's set up housekeepin' for a while."

"I'll drink to that," she said.

"And I'll drink to your drinkin' to that," I said.

And the whiskey went down, full-bodied and warm, spreading through us like life-blood.

Taffy came over and sat on my lap. She ran her long tapering fingers through my hair.

"You know," she said, "I've done a lot of things, but really, I never wanted anything more than this—a little white cottage in the vale, and a good man."

We sat together until darkness enveloped the kitchen. And then we ate by candlelight and went to bed and let our lips and bodies feast on each other until we fell into deep, dreamless sleep while the wind whispered in the ring of the trees and moonlight silvered the down quilt that covered us.

And so the idyll began, a time of innocent days and passionate nights made all the more precious by what we never spoke of. Some days we walked down to the sea and watched the huge waves pound themselves in fury against the shore; some days we walked to the little village and shopped along its single street; and some days we walked high in the foothills and ate fresh bread and cheese and rich Welsh butter and drank wine from a wicker hamper we carried with us.

"It's a beautiful country, Taffy," I said one afternoon as we sat resting after our climb.

"Isn't it, though," she said. "I must have been daft to leave it in the first place. But I always knew I'd come back. I'm glad you could see it, Nick."

"I'm glad I could see it with you," I said.

She clasped my hand. "So am I," she said. "You're sure you aren't bored, though?"

"Bored?" I said. "With a woman like you in a place like this?"

"Well, it's so quiet and peaceful," she said. "You're accustomed to a different sort of life. To being

41

on the move, hunting, being hunted, living in danger and excitement. Playing for big stakes. And then, to come here, where nothing has happened for centuries. Every day is like the one before. The world and its troubles are outside somewhere—they're not in here."

Later I would think of her words and the cruel irony of them. But now I could only laugh and reassure her.

I lay back on the grass and took a deep breath of the clean air carrying a hint of salt from the sea below.

"If this is boredom," I said, "give me more of it. Peace, it's wonderful. Only a fool would grow weary of a place like this."

She moved closer to me and lifted my head into her lap. She was silent for a moment.

"Don't you wish . . ." she said.

But she didn't finish.

"Wish what?" I said.

"Never mind," she said.

But I knew what she had been thinking—that it could go on and on and on.

"Let's eat," she said.

"I've got a better idea,"

"What's that?"

"Let me show you."

And when I did, she agreed that it was a better idea.

And then we had lunch. And then we walked down out of the foothills to the little cottage in the circle of trees.

There was no calendar there, no radio, no television. No mailman came, and no one brought the newspapers. The days came and went, but time seemed to stand still.

But that was a special sort of time in a special sort of world.

In London that night, an Arab oil merchant named Hafez Damu-Bakshishi died. I learned about it later. He had transacted some business with a British corporation at a considerable profit to his firm. And, the investigation showed, he had decided to celebrate with a seventeen-year-old blonde girl, Mavis Keen, who asked—and was to receive—five hundred pounds for her not inconsiderable talents.

Miss Keen described to the police in some detail precisely what services Mr. Damu-Bakshishi had demanded. It was generally agreed that although they were strenuous and not a little bizarre, they were hardly sufficient to have caused her to leave him in the state in which he was found the next day.

Mr. Damu-Bakshishi was found amid the broken furniture and smashed bottles in a courtyard off Wentworth Street in the Stafford Houses, erected by the East End Dwellings Co., Ltd., in 1890. He had been shot three times in the head. The weapon, a Luger was found right beside him.

As I say, I heard about it later. But when it happened, I was in a little world with Taffy Evans, where the days came and went and came again. And each day, the world beyond our vale seemed more remote and unreal, and the tensions that I had known and lived with for so long fled my body and left in their place that full sense of relaxation and satisfaction which is utter peace.

Sometimes it seemed as though Taffy could read my thoughts.

"Do you think there's still a world out there?" she asked one night after dinner as we sat watching the fire.

"No," I said. "It's gone, whirling off somewhere in space with all the fools and maniacs and greedy people."

I think of those words now and number myself among the fools. Poor Taffy. I absolve her. She was entitled to her fantasy. But I should have known better.

We waited until the fire had burned itself down, and when only the glowing embers were left, we retreated to the bedroom and slid beneath the quilt.

My mouth sought hers, and my fingers moved softly on her full breasts and in those secret places that quickened and deepened her breathing.

She threw aside the quilt and, moving her lips away from mine, sent her mouth on a long and lingering exploration of my body. I lay back while she pleasured me with her lips, and then I drew her up beside me again.

She opened her taut thighs and drew me to her, and we began the long, slow exchange of mutual delights.

"Ah," she said. "Ah!"

And the rhythm quickened, and the sighs became helpless moans, and our bodies surged together and apart. Faster, now, faster.

And then she lurched upward and screamed and fell away silent, and in the sliver of moonlight that fell across her exquisite face I could see the dark, bloody pit in her left temple where the silent bullet had entered her brain and stolen what remained of the all-too-short life of Taffy Evans.

I screamed, I remember now. Not a scream of fear,

but more the bellow of a crazed animal. I lurched in fury toward the door, my nostrils wide as though I could somehow smell out the sniper who waited outside. And as I lumbered through the door like some beast with more heart than brain, something heavy smashed across my skull, and as I lapsed into unconsciousness I realized that the pain of that blow was as nothing beside the pain of my loss.

And then there was darkness.

Chapter 6

I awoke to the stench of sweat and the sight of dripping armpits and a pair of immense, swarthy breasts bobbling unappetizingly before me.

A dirty thumb plucked at one of my eyelids. A face moved close to my own. There was a blast of fetid breath. Blotted out were the armpits and the breasts. Instead my vision was filled with the hairy upper lip of a woman, and then her lips parted in what must have been a smile of satisfaction. To me, they revealed only a set of crooked yellow teeth.

The head moved away. I was conscious now of a windowless room with white walls. I was seated, naked, in a wooden chair. My arms and legs were bound to the chair with stout rope that bit into my wrists and ankles. Specks dotted the walls. At first I thought I was seeing spots, and then I realized that what I was seeing were splashes of dried blood.

The bobbling breasts and the armpits sprouting wet black hair crossed my vision again.

I tried to remember what had happened. There were no details. Only sadness, aching loss.

I closed my eyes again.

A hand slashed across my face, snapping my head back and to the side.

My eyes flew open.

Again I saw the yellow teeth and the sadistic smile. The woman had the face of a ferret on the body of a pig.

"Come, my pet," she said. "Come play with Janeen Khasib."

I hoped I was dreaming, hoped it was all a nightmare. I was beginning to remember now—Taffy, dead in my arms; the blinding fury, the mad sprint to the door, the blow on the head.

I closed my eyes again and shook my head to clear it. Again the heavy hand slashed across my face.

"Come, sweet," the fat woman's deep voice said. "Come play with Janeen."

I opened my eyes again. It was no dream. The ferret-faced woman with the porcine body was still standing there. She was naked to the waist. Her pendulous breasts, their dark inverted nipples puckered inside circlets of wiry black hair, bobbled like enormous sausages with her every movement. A lush growth of hair, oily with the constant dripping of her sweat, jutted from under each arm. A thick roll of loose, mottled fat curled over the waistband of her khaki skirt. She wore heavy boots; and under them, encasing the massive pillars of her legs, she wore—incongruously—sheer nylons.

I closed my eyes again.

And again her left hand shot out and slashed across my face.

When I opened my eyes again, I saw something I had not noticed before. It lay open at the far end of the room. A coffin.

"Welcome to Beirut," Janeen Khasib said. "Welcome to the hospitality of the Pan-Arab Protective Society."

"Beirut," I mumbled. "Beirut. It can't be."

Her laugh was as ugly as she was. Thin and shrill, it matched her ferret's face more than her pig's body. A few droplets of sweat broke loose from her armpits and spattered darkly on the cement floor. Her breasts continued to bobble even after her laughter had stopped.

"Yes, Mr. Carter," she said. "It is Beirut. Welcome to the Republique Libanaise. Welcome to the Paris of the Middle East. You are only minutes from the cafés of Hambra Street; only a short distance from the discothèques of the rue de Phoenicie; only a half hour from the gaming tables of the Casino du Liban."

My puzzlement must have been written large on my face. One moment I had been in Wales with a beautiful woman. And now, seemingly next, I was in an almost bare, bloody-walled room with a hideous female.

She gestured toward the coffin.

"Behold," she said. "Your transportation. Britain to Beirut via air freight. Customs men are not too curious about corpses. They are sometimes curious about coffins, but never about corpses. And you, Mr. Carter, with the help of drugs, looked very, very dead."

"So it is Beirut," I said.

She bared her crooked yellow teeth at me in another smile. "Yes. Beirut. Outside are the hotels, the sun-drenched beaches, the beautiful women. But none so beautiful as I—eh, Mr. Carter?''

I said nothing.

Her voice grew insistent. "None so beautiful as I—eh, Mr. Carter?" she repeated.

I stared at her.

She moved closer and, cupping her left hand under my chin, pulled my face up until my eyes locked on hers.

"Say it, Mr. Carter. Say, 'Janeen is beautiful.' ''

I was drenched in the foul odor of her sweat and her fetid breath. I closed my eyes again. Whatever drug they had given me, it was still in my body, tugging me back toward unconsciousness.

Her hand slashed across my face. I snapped to wakefulness.

She covered my mouth with hers, grinding her lips into mine. One of her breasts slithered like a wet bladder over my bare skin.

She broke away and walked behind me. She put her fleshy arms around me. Looking down, I was confronted by a hideous vista of hairy arms, bloated fingers, and dirt-rimmed nails playing over my body.

Her mouth moved close to my ear. "Say it, Mr. Carter," she whispered from behind me. "Say: 'You are lovely, Janeen Khasib. You are the promise of sensual delights. Yours is the body I have always wanted. Yours is the beauty my lust hungers for. I want to take you here on the floor. I want to take the skirt from around your hips. I want to roll down your pink panties. I want to plunge myself between your legs!'"

She broke off momentarily. She was peering over my shoulder, down between my thighs.

Her voice grew angry. "You do not respond to Janeen," she said. "You are like the others, it seems. How sad. How sad that one so handsome as you should not love Janeen."

She moved in front of me. Her eyes were slightly glazed. "But perhaps you are shy," she said. "I will give you one more chance. Come, my pet, say it: 'You are beautiful, Janeen. I could have other women, but it is only you I want. Only your body. Your breasts. Only to be inside you.' "

Her eyes were closed. Her body was swaying. Her hands drew up her wide skirt. Higher, higher. The flesh of her thighs cascaded over the tops of the nylons. A cherry-red garter belt held them up. Tendrils of black hair snaked out of her pink panties. It was obscene. And it was pitiful.

I turned my head away.

She must have sensed the movement. "Filth!" she shrieked. "Filth! You spurn Janeen. Now you will know my wrath."

Her hand flashed behind her skirt, and when it reappeared, something glinted in her fleshy fingers. Over her head, in her right hand, she brandished a bright surgical scalpel.

"You do not wish Janeen?" she said.

Her left hand reached down and gripped my sex. "Then you shall have no woman."

The scalpel was moving directly toward its target. I tried to twist the chair away from her, but it was bolted to the floor.

"Sit still," she hissed.

"Stop!"

For a moment, I thought the voice was my own, a monumental protest, an irresistible command erupting out of anger, revulsion, and torment at this demented woman whose shining blade was inching toward the juncture of my thighs.

But then I realized that the voice had come from behind me, that an unseen door had opened, and that someone with the power to halt the repulsive Janeen had spoken.

Footsteps sounded behind me, and then a man appeared. Janeen looked at him from lowered eyes in a grotesque parody of some provocative flirt.

"For God's sake, Janeen, all I asked you to do was guard him."

"I'm sorry, Muhammad," she said.

"Give me the scalpel, Janeen."

She laid it gently in his upturned palm. She said softly, "Will you give it back, Muhammad, when you are finished with him? Like with the others?"

"Yes, Janeen," he said.

I shuddered despite the heat of the room.

Janeen moved into a corner. The man stood before me. He wore an unadorned military-style khaki shirt and khaki trousers tucked neatly into combat boots. An automatic pistol—it looked like one of the .32-caliber Model Ds turned out by the Manufacture d'Armes Automatiques of Bayonne, France—was jammed under his belt.

His face was thin, and his eyes burned with an intensity that suggested fanaticism.

"Permit me to apologize for Janeen," he said. "She is not without her uses to the Pan-Arab Protective Society. But I am afraid that she has given you a misleading impression."

His voice became little more than a whisper. "Janeen's need for us is—how shall I put it?—rather psychosexual. Our need for Janeen at this point in our rather brief existence is rather mercenary. She is quite wealthy. In time, as our cause becomes better established and funds flow in from other sources, her support will become less essential and her role, I expect, less visible. But for the moment she is vital to us. So we indulge her. But do not let her behavior encourage you to believe, Mr. Carter, that we of the Pan-Arab Protective Society are frivolous fools with our brains between our legs. No indeed. No indeed. I trust you agree."

I shrugged.

"Oh, come now, Mr. Carter. Surely such a renowned operative as yourself—AXE Killmaster, are you not?—could be a bit more generous in your assessment of this fledgling organization of mine. An organization so new that I daresay even AXE has no record of it in its files."

I stared up at him noncommittally. But what he said was true.

"After all," he continued, "it is no mean feat to have captured an AXE Killmaster such as yourself, a man who has escaped death many times, a man who has brushed with every intelligence organization in the world—and survived."

He laughed. "But not this time. This time you shall pay for your crimes. And the world will know of it."

He reached down and grabbed me by the hair. "Know of it! Know of it! Know of it!" he shrieked.

"For the first time I spoke. "Suppose you just calm down and tell me what this is about, Mr. . . . " I said.

"Mister?" He threw back his head and laughed. Then he pushed his face close to mine. "I am a general," he said. "A general and the commander-in-chief of the Pan-Arab Protection Society."

He clicked his heels. It wasn't the time to ponder where he had picked up that little affectation.

"I am General Muhammad Shan-al-Nassim."

"Fine," I said. "You know who I am. I know who you are. Now suppose you tell me what I am doing here."

His hand darted out and slapped me across the face. "I expected no less of you," he said. "I knew you would pretend to be innocent—at least at first. But in time, you will decide differently. You will make a confession. And why will you make a confession? Because if you confess, we will give you a treat. And do you know what the treat is?"

"Tell me," I said.

"The treat is death," he said. "Yes, the time will come with us when you will look upon death as a treat. And you have my word—we will give it to you if you confess."

"Well," I said, "it all sounds very promising, Muhammad."

He slammed the back of his hand across my lips. I tasted blood.

"I like to be called General by the enemies of the Arab people," he said. "The Pan-Arab Protective Society isn't one of these fringe terrorist groups run by fanatics. We may be new and somewhat small, but we must be reckoned with, Mr. Carter. And your confession will elevate us into the front ranks of those who serve the Arab people."

"Well, maybe I'd like to help you," I said, "but I can't very well confess if I don't know what I'm supposed to have done."

Muhammad Sham-al-Nassim looked at his watch. "Please don't waste my time," he said. "Janeen, go get the equipment."

"Yes, Muhammad," she said.

She returned in a moment, dragging a small table. Laid out on it were a few batteries, some thin wire, a box of matches and a cigar, a few pairs of pliers, a couple of hypodermic syringes—a sort of beginner's torture kit. And in the middle of it all, a tape recorder.

Janeen retreated to a corner of the room, crossed her arms over the misshapen sausages of her breasts, licked her lips, and waited.

Muhammad perched on the edge of the table. "Let us begin, Mr. Carter." He switched on the tape recorder. He put a match to the cigar and sucked it into glowing life. I strained my wrists against the ropes binding me to the chair. Whoever had tied me had done a good job.

Muhammad put the end of the cigar to the tip of one of the pieces of wire and blew. It glowed red, then white.

"Tell me how it began," he said.

"How what began?"

He touched the glowing wire to the inside of my

thigh. There were the odor of seared flesh, a rising wisp of smoke, a charred dot, and an agonizing spear of pain. My straining body brought the ropes chafing deeply into my wrists and ankles.

Muhammad smiled at me. "Please, Mr. Carter," he said. "Do not play us for fools. We know everything."

"Splendid," I said. "I'm sorry I can't make the same statement."

Muhammad sucked again on the cigar and set the thin wire to glowing. This time he raked it along my thigh, leaving a trail of blistered flesh. He was beginning to make the repulsive Janeen seem angelic.

"I suppose there are even more sophisticated devices," Muhammad mused. "Perhaps someday, when the Pan-Arab Protective Society is more firmly established as the defender of our people, we shall have them. But I will always prefer these little wires. So tiny. So easy to insert in interesting places."

It was ironic. I thought of the many times I had withheld secrets under duress. And now, even if I wanted to tell this megalomaniacal sadist something, there was nowhere to begin. What did he want? And why?

"I have no wish to prolong your agony, Mr. Carter," he said. "I have no wish to waste my own valuable time. Perhaps you believe we are bluffing. We are not. We know everything."

I shook my head angrily.

"You think not?" he said. "You think we are some upstart Palestinian organization, all bluster and idiocy?"

He threw back his head and laughed.

"I will tell you what, Mr. Carter, Mr. AXE Killmaster N3. Out of respect for your awesome reputation, as a final tribute to a career well-known to all the world's intelligenne organizations, and to shorten your agony, I will help you along."

"Fine," I said.

"Remember, now," Muhammad said. "We know what you have done. What we need to know is why. You have committed crimes against the Arab people."

I raised my eyebrows.

"Yes," he said. "On the fifth day of May, flight 812 operated by Pan American Airways left Djakarta. Among the passengers was yourself. In the dossiers of all self-respecting intelligence organizations—I used to be an intelligence officer myself—is a file on an American agent known for his use of three weapons—a Luger, a stilletto, and a small gas bomb. That agent, Mr. Carter, is you.

"Also aboard flight 812 was one Malik Jabal-Zahab, a high official of Confreres Saudi, a major concern dealing in that most precious of commodities, crude oil. Mr. Jabal-Zahab had just arranged the sale of a large quantity of oil to French interests based in Djakarta. When flight 812 landed in Los Angeles, Mr. Jabal-Zahab was found dead under a blanket. The instrument of death? A poison gas."

"I didn't do it," I said.

Muhammad Sham-al-Nassim flicked the wire across my face.

"Please be quiet until I am finished," he said. "On May the twentieth, in London, a Mr. Hafez Damu-Bakshishi, also a high executive of an oil company, completed a major sale of that precious commodity to British interests. Mr. Damu-Bakshishi thought he would mark the occasion by partaking of the pleasures of a woman. Someone trailed him to his rendezvous, waited outside until Mr. Damu-Bakshishi had sated himself, and then killed him and dumped his body in a squalid courtyard. The instrument of death? A Luger.''

I opened my mouth to protest my innocence, but before I could speak, Muhammad raised his hand to forestall me.

''Two crimes against the Arab people,'' he went on. ''In each case, the weapon is one associated with only one intelligence operative in the world.''

''Doesn't it seem a little too pat to you?'' I said. ''Doesn't it seem a little odd that everything is so neat? That in the first case I kill someone on a plane where it is easy to trace the passengers? That in the second case I leave my pistol behind?''

Muhammad smiled a smile of infinite Levantine wisdon. ''That is the beauty part, is it not, Mr. Carter? The clues so obvious that most people would assume that it could not be—that you would not be so clumsy. But we of the Pan-Arab Protective Society saw through that brilliant stratagem. After that, it became a matter of running you to ground, of finding you in your hiding place. The murder in London was a mistake. We have many friends there. There was no indication that you had left the country. We were able to find records of your arrival, of your purchase of tickets to the remoteness of Wales. The rest took a few days, but it was simple.''

I thought again of Taffy, poor, doomed Taffy, with

her head blown open—robbed of whatever last few days she had been entitled to. My face darkened with anger. I felt the blood surging through me. I made a silent vow to get whoever had set me up for Muhammad.

Muhammad must have been reading my thoughts. "The girl was something of an impediment. So as a professional, you will understand that she had to be eliminated."

"You miserable bastard," I said.

Muhammad chuckled. "Poor Mr. Carter. I am afraid we interrupted a pleasant interlude when we eliminated the girl. Was she very good?"

I wanted to kill him. My body convulsed against the ropes. It was futile.

"Bringing you back here was a rather simple matter, Mr. Carter," Muhammad said. "We knew what you had done. The only remaining question before we disposed of you was why. Why did your government order you to move against our people?"

"I had nothing to do with those killings," I said.

"Come now, Mr. Carter," Muhammad said. "The killings are past history. They are not in dispute. The question again is, why?"

Muhammad had picked up the cigar again and flicked off the ash. He was blowing on the tip, his breath fanning the tobacco into a brilliant orange glow. Once again, he held one of the thin wires to the end of the cigar.

"Why," he asked, "did the United States government, which employs you, order the elimination of two Arab oil executives? What did these men have in common? I will tell you. At a time of acute oil shortages in the Western World, both had made major sales to countries other than the United States. American companies had been bidding on this oil, but they were outbid—in the one case by a French concern; in the other by British interests. So I suggest to you that your government decided to intimidate my people, to suggest to them that it would be unhealthy in the future not to favor American business.''

"Preposterous," I said.

Muhammad laughed. "Perhaps your superiors do not entrust you with their motivations," Mr. Carter. "Perhaps I was mistaken in believing that a superior agent such as yourself would be made privy to strategy. Perhaps you are but an ignorant mercenary out to kill with no knowledge of why. If that is the case, then your usefulness to us is extremely limited—as is your future.''

"If you're trying to appeal to my pride or my cowardice, you're wasting your time," I said. "I didn't kill either of the oil dealers. There is no strategy of intimidation. I have nothing to confess to you. And if you have any plans for me, you'd better get on with them. I'm sick of your talk and your cheap torture.''

"What is that American slogan?" Muhammed asked. "Ah, yes: 'Have it your way.' So be it, Mr. Carter—have it your way. Whether you knew the strategy or not, I would still like to have your confession. Broadcast on our clandestine radio to the Arab people, it will mobilize them to eradicate American influence from the Middle East. And when American influence is eliminated from this part of the world, it will be simple for our people to reclaim the lands now occupied by the Israelis.

"The Middle East is for the Arabs, Mr. Carter, not for the Israelis and their American friends. So come, let us be about our business. I am going to apply various instruments to your body, Mr. Carter. I will not bother to bargain further with you. This is not the marketplace. I will apply the instruments. And when you are ready, simply begin to talk. The tape recorder is running. Confess that you killed these two men on orders of your government to intimidate the Arab people. And then, as I promised, you will be allowed to die."

And so—with evident pleasure, he began, moving up from the soles of my feet with his array of primitive devices. In a corner of the room, her mouth slightly agape, her tiny eyes feasting on my agony, Janeen Khasib stood, waiting like a hyena for my ravaged carcass to become her prey. Muhammad smiled and hummed as he went about his work.

He was above the knees, working his way toward my crotch, when I awoke the second time from blessed unconsciousness. The first blackout had been brief; the second, longer. It was only a matter of time before I passed over into a special realm that knew no pain at all. Muhammad was an amateur. He would overdo it. He would overplay his hand. He would release me from all pain. I would be dead before the hideous Janeen could play out her fantasies on my mutilated body.

I closed my eyes and tried to blot out the sight of him and the sense of what he was doing. I sent one thought through my mind in rhythmic pulses: "Say nothing . . . say nothing . . . say nothing."

In the room, all was silent save for the occasional whir of Muhammad's battery, the hiss of burning flesh, the occasional shuffling of Janeen's booted feet as she shifted her position, and the rasp of her excited breath as it erupted from under her pendulous breasts, through her throat, and over her sharp yellow teeth.

And then, through the haze of pain that engulfed me, I heard a muffled noise. My eyes flickered open. I saw Muhammad look up, startled. I saw Janeen start from her end of the room toward the door somewhere behind me.

Muhammad backed away from me and tugged the MAB automatic out of his belt.

A door burst open. Gunfire crackled. Muzzle blast exploded close to my ear. I saw the MAB automatic go sliding across the floor. Another shot. Then, ever so slowly, Janeen staggered backward into my line of vision, staring incredulously at her chest. A heavy double stream of blood was pulsing out of a small hole, drenching her mammoth breasts. She backpedaled across the floor in what looked like a slow-motion response to the impact of the bullet, and then, crashing up against the far wall, she slid to the floor. Her skirt had rucked up over her elephantine thighs. The blood from her breast dripped down onto her cherry-red garter belt and the pale flab billowing over the tops of her nylon stockings. Then her eyes closed. The woman with the face of a ferret on the body of a pig was dead. In death as in life, Janeen Khasib was as pitiful as she was grotesque.

Behind me, I heard a somewhat breathless voice say, "Are we in time?"

A woman's voice answered, "Yes, he's still alive."

In the next moment, a beautiful, long-legged, dark-haired girl dressed in khaki slacks and a tight T-shirt that stretched across her full, firm breasts stood before me. The pistol in her hand seemed incongruous.

I wanted to smile. My brain seemed sluggish.

She stared down at my nakedness. I felt my body responding to her.

"Yes," I heard her say, "he's very much alive."

And then darkness crept over me, a strange whirlpool of unconsciousness, swirling with the faces of Taffy and Hawk, Janeen and Muhammad, and the magnificent dark-haired girl with the luscious body.

When I awoke this time, it was to the scent of sea air, the pulse of a ship's engine, and the sight of a life vest lettered with the ship's name and port. *"Miranda Jordan,"* it said. "Haifa."

I swung myself out of the below-decks berth. Someone had gone to work on the results of Muhammad's experiments with torture. The repairs had been skillful.

Through an open hatch on the small boat I could see a patch of blue sky. A moment later, a face looked down at me, and then a lanky, fair-haired man dropped nimbly through the opening, landed in front of me, smiled, and stuck out his hand.

"Zev Tzion," he said. "Israeli intelligence. Pleased to meet you, Carter."

I gripped his hand. "So I owe my life to the 'Institute,' " I said, using the little-known nickname of the special branch of Mossad organized to conduct anti-terrorist operations.

He sat down on the bunk opposite me. "Well, don't

be too quick with the gratitude,'' he said, still smiling. ''Rescuing you wasn't an entirely altruistic act on our part. We are expecting something more in return than mere thanks, you know. But I must say it was a personal pleasure to bail you out. I've read about you in our files—and our files are among the best, I assure you. I think maybe we owe you a few favors too, but don't tell anyone I said so.''

''If silence is the beginning of repayment,'' I said, ''I'm happy to comply.''

''Let's say that settles any personal debt you think you owe me.''

''More than generous of you,'' I said.

''But my government has more demanding ideas.''

''Yes,'' I said, smiling back at him. ''Governments usually do. But tell me, how did you manage to get me out of the fix I was in?''

Zev Tzion put a match to a cigarette he took from a pack in the breast pocket of his short-sleeved shirt.

''If you feel well enough,'' he said, ''let's go up on deck where there's a breeze to blow away the smoke.''

He led me topside, and as we broke through into the clean sea air and the brilliant sunshine glistening on the even swells of the Mediterranean, I saw that we were aboard a fishing smack.

In the wheelhouse amidships, the dark-haired girl—her back toward me—was at the helm.

Zev and I walked toward the stern, where he lowered a hinged board that passed for a bench. A moment later, a bearded man walked up, handed Zev a vacuum jug of coffee, and departed.

''Thanks, Uri,'' Zev called after him.

Zev took a final drag on his cigarette, tossed the butt out into the breeze, and watched it carried away safely into the sea.

He poured some coffee for each of us and said, "Actually, it was just a lucky break that we were able to save you. The "Institute" wasn't looking for you. We just happened to stumble on you in the course of other work."

I laughed. "Well, so much for any egotistical thoughts I might have had that my disappearance had set off an international search."

"The truth is that our agents in Beirut had been conducting a surveillance of the Pan-Arab Protection Society. It is, or shall I say was, a new organization. Outfits like it are popping up all the time, but this one seemed worth taking a bit more seriously than some of the others. Your friend Muhammad is a former intelligence officer."

"Yes," I said, "he told me that."

"And not really a bad one," Zev continued. "He gave us a few sticky moments in the past. But he was dismissed from the army a couple of years ago. Being a more than ordinarily zealous pan-Arabist, he had a tendency to get mixed up with violently radical groups plotting the overthrow of the Lebanese government and the installation of regimes committed to a union of all Arab nations to apply the most extreme actions against Israel. Once he was thrown out of the army, he decided that the only way to bring about what he wanted was to start an organization of his own."

I nodded as Zev continued.

"Four things made him especially dangerous: a military background with some expertise in intelligence; a knowledge of what had caused similar radical movements to fail; sufficient personal presence to attract a loyal cadre that would carry out his orders and bring in recruits; and, most of all, money.''

"That," I said, "was the contribution of Janeen Khasib.''

"Precisely," Zev said.

Cupping his hands around the flame to shield it from the brisk breeze that whipped back our hair, Zev Tzion put a match to another cigarette.

"It was the money that made him especially formidable. Money to buy weapons. Money to pay bribes. Money to buy loyalty. Money to pull off an operation like the one that brought you to Beirut.''

"The logistical part of it seems to have gone off well," I said. "The overall plan wasn't bad, and if I had given him what he wanted—the confession to a couple of murders I didn't commit—he might have made it embarrassing for my government.''

"And given a shot in the arm besides to the Arab factions that cannot bring themselves to accept that living in peace with Israel makes sense for everyone in this part of the world.''

"But I still don't know how you came to move in on Muhammad.''

Zev took a puff on his cigarette.

"It was the coffin," he said. "We had Muhammad's headquarters under surveillance. And then one day we received a report that a coffin had been carried inside. It was clear from the weight of it—several men were needed to carry it—that someone, or something, was inside.''

Zev paused.

"I must tell you the truth," he said. "The someone did not matter to us as much as the *something*—the possibility that what was inside was weaponry. Poison gas. Automatic arms. Small missiles. Explosives. The ingredients for nuclear devices."

Up ahead, I could see land.

"Haifa," Zev said before continuing. "The time seemed ripe for us to move in. We knew Muhammad was inside. We knew eventually we would have to eliminate him before he tried to eliminate us. The chance that he was about to engineer something that would make him more difficult for us to deal with in the future made us decide to act. We had the boat waiting—I assure you it had a name and home port vastly different from the one you saw belowdecks—so our escape route was secure. And we knew that besides Muhammad and Janeen, there was only a handful of his people in the house where they brought the coffin. The rest was not especially difficult."

The *Miranda Jordan* was slowing down now, nosing her way into the busy port. In the wheelhouse I could see the dark-haired girl maneuvering it with unaffected ease.

"But once you got me out of there, how did you know it was me?"

Zev smiled. "I told you our files were good."

The boat was pulling alongside a pier, where a man in a sailor's cap was waiting. The bearded man who had brought us the coffee tossed him a rope, and the dark-haired girl maneuvered the *Miranda Jordan* skillfully into its berth.

"One other thing," I said to Zev.

"Yes?"

"The girl—who is she?"

"I think you'd better call her Leila. Leila Jamilat."

"That's an Arab name," I said.

"Yes. It means beautiful night."

"It fits her well," I said.

"It's not her real name. But you'd better get used to calling her that."

I looked at him in surprise.

He reached into the pocket where he kept his cigarettes. "I have a message for you from Hawk." He handed me a slip of paper rolled like a cigarette.

I undid the tiny scroll.

The message consisted of five words written over Hawk's signature. "Meet me among the dead," it said.

Chapter 7

At the best of times, it is an eerie place. At a minute after midnight, when no tourist is likely to wander through, it is a chill and grisly site. In the dim light, I looked up at the ceiling. A skeleton, clutching a scythe made of human bone, stared down at me out of sockets that had known no eyes for centuries.

In the rear wall of the crypt, erect mummies, clothed in brown robes, seemed to nod like weary guards in sentry boxes decorated with the fleshless underpinning of human bodies dead perhaps four hundred years. And as if off-duty, two robed skeletons reclined on a bed of bones beneath a skull-topped arch set against either wall.

Bones were everywhere: pieces of pelvis, arranged in decorative piles; neat bits of vertebrae stretched into designs that filigreed the walls and ceilings. Besides myself, in that odd little room, the only living things were a few pots of flowers.

The Italians call it the Cimitero dei Cappuchini, the cemetery of the Capuchins. It is one of the strangest places in all the world, an underground passage in the heart of Rome about 130 feet long consisting of a corridor and six arched compartments adorned by some unknown artists with the bones of four thousand capuchin monks who died between 1528 and 1870.

Hawk had picked it for our meeting place. *Well,* I thought, as I waited, *it does have a central location, right on the Via Veneto.*

What Hawk had used in his message to me was a standard AXE tertiary emergency code, memorized by all agents and used to set up rendezvous in any of the major cities of the world. "Meet me next to the sky," for example, would have set up a meeting at the Eiffel Tower in Paris. All meetings were scheduled for just after midnight local time.

So the message wasn't unusual. What was out of the ordinary was that it was sent by Hawk himself, for a meeting on foreign soil with Hawk himself. What had brought the old fox out of his lair on Dupont Circle?

I knew I wouldn't have long to wait. Tertiary-emergency-code rendezvous is set for 12:01 A.M. If the rendezvous is not kept within ten minutes, it is canceled and must be rescheduled.

I looked around again at the skeletons in the vault, and I read from a little brochure I had picked up on the way in: "The little crosses that mark the resting places of the dead, and the mummified remains, in a standing or recumbent position, remind the visitors of the drama of life, which ends in death, while the fantastic designs worked out in human bones, on the walls of the arches, invite to prayer and meditation."

There was a hideous beauty about the place, I had to

concede. I thought again of poor Taffy—a victim of the drama of life, which ends in death.

And then the odor of damp was intruded upon by another smell. Looking down the corridor I could see the glow of his cigar and, a moment later, Hawk.

He carried a bundle under one arm. With the other he gestured at the skeletons and bits of bone. "Interesting place, isn't it?" he said through his cigar.

'A bit on the depressing side."

"That's why I picked it. All this death around. Keeps people on their toes. Reminds them how they're going to end up if they're not careful. Does more good than a hundred lectures."

He held out the bundle to me. "Here, dammit. Take this."

I unwrapped the package. Inside were Wilhelmina, Hugo, and Pierre.

"The British sent them back," Hawk said. "Old friends of mine in MI6. Picked them up from the local police after that girl was found dead in Wales. What the hell happened up there?"

I told him, omitting the more intimate details. When I started in on the part about the Israeli agents bursting into Muhammad's setup, he gestured me into silence.

"I know about that, dammit. That's why I'm here."

Hawk flicked the ash from his cigar into a flowerpot.

"Something's up," he said. "It worries me. It worries the Israelis. Someone tries to frame you for putting away two oil merchants. Arabs. Someone wants Arab zealots to believe an AXE agent carried out the murder of two Arabs on instructions of the U.S. government. And what stirs up the Arabs interests the Israelis."

"Any idea who?" I said.

"No, but it obviously involves oil. And these days, to the industrialized nations of the world, oil is like blood. Cut off the supply, and you die. We've got to find out what's going on. And the Israelis want in on it. They got me here. They sent word that they had picked up one of my people—you—and that the price for safe return was their participation in any operation you were engaged in affecting their part of the world. I didn't have much choice. They're tough. But we've done business together before. They're good people. The only place where I drew the line was when they wanted me to come to Israet. That might have been impolitic. So we compromised on Rome as the site for working out the details and picking you up."

"I suppose you've already started the ball rolling," I said.

"That's right."

"They've nominated their agent?"

"We've sketched out the outline of the operation."

"Just fine," I said, with a slight edge to my voice.

Hawk appeared not to notice. "And we have every hope that it's going to smoke out whoever has been trying to frame Nick Carter and, through Nick Carter, the United States government. Now I want to get cracking on this. The Israelis are all set to go. I've got some people from Special Effects here in Rome waiting to go to work on you. These murders are just the tip of the iceberg. Someone out there has some volatile ideas. I don't know what they are, but I think we'd better find out fast."

"I'm all for that," I said. "But maybe you're tying my hands."

Hawk put a match to another cigar and looked up at me. "What do you mean?"

"This business of working with the Israelis. Nobody knows better than I what we owe them, but I'd rather go it alone."

"I made a deal with them," Hawk said through his cigar. "And somehow," he said, taking a last look around, "I feel it in my bones that you're not going to mind."

Chapter 8

The flashbulbs started popping the moment we stepped off the Alitalia jet at Heathrow Airport in London.

"Hold it," a voice yelled up from the pack of photographers. "Hold it right there on the ramp. Give us the legs, lady."

"Nuzzle up to the sheikh a little, honey."

"That's right. Smile."

"Hold it. I want one more."

The shutters kept clicking. Television cameramen elbowed one another for position. Airline officials and airport personnel made half-hearted efforts at shooing the newsmen off.

"Put your arm around her, Sheikh."

"No, wait a minute. Your robes are in the way of her legs. Give us the legs, sweetie. And those big titties, too," the photographer mumbled.

"Please, please," one of the airport people said. "Let the sheikh off. We've set up facilities for a news conference in the VIP lounge. If you'll all please go there, we can get started right away."

"Bugger off," yelled one of the photographers.

"Look here—"

The photographer pushed him out of the way.

"Look over here," came another voice. "Right this way. That's right. That's right." A shutter clicked. "Beautiful!"

A bespectacled little man with thin blonde hair slicked back over his pink scalp tugged at the tails of his cutaway, hitched up his striped trousers, and made his way up the ramp.

"Basil Goodfellow," he said. "At your service. I'm sorry about this, Your Highness. We had hoped to keep them confined the the VIP lounge. But newsmen are like animals. Especially the ones who take the pictures. And among them, especially the ones from television. I'll try to clear this up."

He stood in front of me and raised his arms. "All right," he said.

"Out of the way, dammit, I'm trying to work."

Basil Goodfellow persisted. "Now look," he said to the mob waiting down below, "if you'll simply go into the lounge, I'll bring the sheikh to you in a few minutes."

"Screw off, Basil, you bloody sod."

Basil's pale face flushed. He turned to me. "I'm sorry, Your Highness," he said. "They seem more than ordinarily stirred up today. I don't know what it is."

"Let's see more of the legs, sweetie," a voice called. "Pull your skirt up a little."

Basil flushed again. "If you'll forgive me, I suspect it's your wife. Look, why don't you go back inside the aircraft for a few minutes. I'll try to get them calmed down."

I did my best to look a trifle put out by it all. "Very well," I said.

Basil ushered us inside. When he went outside again, I could hear his high-pitched voice at work. "All right, you bastards. Get in the lounge and wait."

"Up yours, Basil," someone shouted.

I did my best not to laugh.

He was back in less than five minutes, slightly out of breath, tugging his vintage cutaway and striped trousers into place as he reboarded the plane.

He rubbed his hands together. "There, now," he said. "I think everything's quite in order. If you'll be so good as to accompany me, Your Highness and madam."

He led us across into one of the main arrivals buildings. "Don't worry about the customs formalities. They're being taken care of for you."

"Splendid," I said.

"Now I'm going to take you into the VIP lounge. The press will be waiting for you there again. If you'd like, we can make other arrangements for madam—Her Highness—while you deal with the press."

"No," I said. "She will accompany me."

"As you wish, sir," Basil said, as we strode briskly down a long corridor while jets roared in and out above us.

A conference table had been set up on a dais for us. Several microphones were already in place, and as we seated ourselves, the hot television lights glared on. I reached inside my robe and extracted a large pair of dark glasses.

"Tell him to take them off," I heard someone say.

"No," came the reply. "Let him leave them on.

75

They make him look like one of those really sinister wogs.''

Basil leaned into the thicket of microphones. His voice rang metallically through the room. "Ladies and gentlemen," he said, "may I present to you Sheikh Sharif Sultan al-Qadi.''

Basil started to step back from the microphones.

"Don't be a sexist, Basil," said a woman's voice.

Basil leaned back into the microphones. "And Mrs. al-Qadi.''

"What's her first name?''

Basil looked flustered.

"Leila," I said.

A momentary hush fell over the room.

Basil faded away.

"Your Highness," said a voice from the back of the room, "we have been led to believe that you are here to sell oil on behalf of an independent syndicate in control of substantial Middle Eastern reserves.

"That is correct," I said.

"I was under the impression that the Organization of Petroleum Exporting Countries—OPEC—was in control of all oil coming out of that area.''

"I am afraid that is not correct," I said.

There was a buzz throughout the room.

One reporter left his seat and bolted out of the room.

A new voice rang out: "Are you telling us that you are in competition with OPEC?''

"No, not necessarily. I am simply representing a number of individuals who control substantial reserves that are not committed to OPEC. We are not in competition with OPEC. We are simply an alternative to

OPEC. We are businessmen. We have something to sell."

"Over here," a voice said.

A tall young man was on his feet, waving his upraised hand to catch my eye.

"I've checked with some of my sources. They say they've never heard of you."

The room was hushed. I leaned into the microphone.

"That's unfortunate," I said. I could feel the tension rising. "I suggest you get yourself some new sources."

There was a burst of laughter. The worst was over.

"What do you call those robes, Sheikh?" a voice said.

"An *abayeh*," I replied. "The long cotton garment beneath it is a *thawb*. The headdress, I am sure you are familiar with."

"How come your wife dresses differently?"

It was Leila's turn to divert them. "I prefer Western clothing," she said.

"Thank God for that!" someone shouted. There was more laughter.

I welcomed it. The reporters were willing to be diverted, to turn the news conference into an amusing circus that would spare them the hard work of trying to find out more about Sheikh Sharif Sultan al-Qadi and the impact of his oil on the world's economy.

"Does your husband object to those short skirts?" came another voice.

"Do you?" Leila asked.

"Hell, no," came the reply. More laughter.

"My husband, upon occasion, prefers Western dress himself," Leila said.

"With someone like you, why bother to dress at all?" someone mumbled loudly.

There were a few snickers.

"How long do you expect to be in London?"

"As long as it takes me to conduct my business," I said.

"Then your oil has not been sold?"

"It has been bid upon, but not sold," I said.

"What is the extent of the reserves you control?"

"Let me put it this way: less than the amount controlled by Saudi Arabia. Less than the amount controlled by Iran and Kuwait. Less than the amount controlled by Iraq. Less than the amount controlled by the United Arab Emirates. But more than the total controlled by Qatar, Bahrain and Oman."

"What you're saying, then, is: more than twelve billion barrels and less than twenty four billion."

"You are saying it, my good man. But I compliment you on your knowledge of statistics."

Basil Goodfellow was hovering at my elbow.

"Gentlemen, gentlemen," he said, "the sheikh and his wife have had a long flight. Let's think about cutting this short."

Hands were still waving down below me. I pointed to one.

"Will you be spending all your time here on business?"

"No," I said. "I am afraid that my wife would find that very dull indeed. Actually, it would make me quite happy to conclude my business swiftly. London has always been a favorite of ours. And I am most anxious to partake of the many pleasures here."

"What about you, Mrs.—er—al-Qadi?"

"I hope to do some shopping," Leila said. "I hope to visit your theater. I hope to dine at some of your fine restaurants. I hope to go dancing, perhaps, although the sheikh is not so fond as I of your popular music."

"Well, you can dance with me any time," said one of the voices.

Leila pushed back her chair. "Perhaps the occasion will arise," she said.

She rose gracefully, and her presence was such that the reporters accepted that the conference was over. There were some last efforts at picture taking.

Technicians came up to the table and began switching off and disconnecting the microphones. The glaring lights of the television crews went dead. In three minutes the room was empty except for the two of us and Basil. Cigarette butts littered the floor. Someone had spilled a cup of coffee over one of the chairs.

"Animals," Basil Goodfellow said. "They're animals."

"Not very deadly, I would venture," I said.

Basil chuckled appreciatively. "No, indeed, sir, no indeed. Annoying sometimes, but not very deadly. I must remember that next time they act up."

Basil rubbed his hands together.

"Now, sir, is there anything I can get you or Her Highness? Some tea, perhaps?"

"No, thank you," I said.

He rubbed his hands some more. "Well, then, I suppose you'll be wanting your car now. I understand a car has been laid on for you. If you'll just wait right here, I'll see to it. I'll have your luggage put in the boot.

I'll pick up your passports for you. I'll attend to everything, and then I'll just hurry back here and get the two of you and show you the way out.''

He began backing out of the room, half-bowing as he went. ''So if you'll just wait right here, sir and madam, I'll be back as quickly as I can.''

Basil managed to back out of the room without falling over anything.

I took off the dark glasses.

Lelila sighed. ''I'm glad that's over,'' she said.

''That makes two of us.''

''Do you think they bought it?''

''We'll know by the time we get to our hotel,'' I said.

The papers would be out then with the story of the arrival of Sheikh Sharif Sultan al-Qadi—if they thought it was news. In Rome, Hawk had sketched out the plan: to masquerade as a sheikh, to use Leila as his wife, to go to London, a center of international trade and the site of one of the murders, to appear to have a large, somewhat uncommitted supply of oil, and to see whether anyone was prepared to kill because of it.

Men from Special Effects had worked on me for hours. My skin was darkened, my nose lengthened slightly and curved like the blade of a scimitar. A black mustache and beard and the Arab garb completed the transformation of Nick Carter into Sheikh Sharif Sultan al-Qadi.

As for the girl known as Leila, the Israeli sun had already endowed her skin with the soft color of light coffee. All they had done was to outfit her as was befitting the wife of a wealthy oil dealer.

It meant a busy day in the best boutiques of Rome—

dresses from La Mendola, shoes from Ferragamo, jewelry from Bulgari, handbags and sportswear from Gucci. For me, there were a couple of suits from Brioni. Between us, thanks to the masquerade and the treasuries of two nations, we had ten pieces of Vuitton luggage when we boarded the Alitalia jet for London at Leonardo da Vinci International Airport. Someone was going to be mighty angry if the masquerade was blown within minutes of our arrival in London.

Basil Goodfellow poked his head through the door. "Your car is waiting," he said.

Leila and I followed him down a corridor. At the end of it, a compact-looking Japanese dressed in a black chauffeur's uniform bared his teeth in a smile of welcome and then delivered himself of a crisp bow.

"Your Highness," he said, "permit me to introduce myself. I am your chauffeur. My name is Minoru. I am at your service during your stay. Day and night. Anything you wish, anyplace you care to go, simply summon Minoru. Same thing for your lady."

"Thank you," I said.

"And now I take you to your car. All your luggage is aboard."

Even if I had been a sheikh, I would have been impressed with the car. A prewar Rolls-Royce P-III limousine—long, black, and luxurious. Gleaming. Spotless. An unmistakable symbol of wealth.

Minoru opened a door and beckoned us inside. "I take you now to your hotel, yes?" he said.

I nodded at him.

Leila and I settled ourselves in the smooth leather seats. Before us, in a burnished wood case, sat three crystal decanters of scotch, brandy, and sherry. In fitted insets was an array of glasses.

Minoru climbed into the front seat, and we began rolling noiselessly toward central London.

"Pleasant auto, isn't it?" I said, as though I spent every day riding in luxury.

Leila shot a glance at me. "Quite pleasant, sire," she said, entering into the spirit of things.

"Bit of sherry?" I said.

"Don't mind," she said.

"Splendid," I said.

We toasted each other in fine crystal and finer sherry. The trip into town went by rapidly.

A sprawling three-room suite was awaiting us at Claridge's. When the retinue of servants that ushered us and our luggage up had finally vanished, I checked it out for hidden microphones. It was clean, I told Leila. And then I picked up the telephone.

"Will you send up all the newspapers," I said.

They arrived, notably crisp, in a matter of seconds. I spewed them across the bed. London's press had not lost its competitive speed or its taste for sensationalism.

"Will you look at that!" Leila exclaimed.

It was page 1 in every one of them.

"Mystery Sheikh Arrives, Selling Non—OPEC Oil," one of them blared.

Taking up the rest of the page was an enormous photograph with heavy emphasis on Leila's miniskirted legs. The other papers were not very different.

"I'd say it's a success," she said.

"It looks that way—thanks to you," I told her. "You saved me a lot of trouble, diverting them the way you did. I was pretty well briefed in Rome, but I don't think I would have liked answering questions about oil all day.''

Leila bent her head so that her shimmering black hair fell about her face. Looking up at me, she said, ''It is a wife's pleasure to serve her sheikh.''

''In all ways and at all times?'' I said.

I reached out and drew her close to me. Her breathing grew rapid. Her full breasts heaved against the sheer fabric of her blouse.

''Yes,'' she whispered.

I reached for the telephone. ''Sheikh Sultan Sharif al-Qadi here,'' I announced. ''I wish all calls held until further notice. I wish two buckets of your finest champagne.''

We did not have long to wait. Silver buckets beaded with frost held the green bottles. The waiter bowed himself out of the room.

''Your sheikh is tired after his travels,'' I told Leila. ''He wishes cold drinks, a bath, and the pleasures of his wife.''

Leila smiled up at me. ''I will draw your bath,'' she said. She carried the buckets into the bathroom. I heard water running in the tub.

''It is ready, Your Highness,'' she called.

When I entered, she was waiting for me. In the tub. Naked.

''I think you'll find the temperature to your liking,'' she said, holding out a glass of champagne.

I reached down, cupped one of her large, firm breasts in my hand, and kissed her upturned lips. She moaned softly and sent her tongue darting at mine.

I shucked off my Arab garments.

"Hurry," she said. She was leaning over the side of the tub, kissing the traces of Muhammad's torture on my thighs. "Hurry, my sheikh, to your Leila."

She did not have to ask again.

She thrust up out of the water like some breathtaking Venus arising from the waves. And I met her body with my own.

When it was over, we made our way to the bed and slept, wrapped in each other's bodies, for the rest of the afternoon.

We finished the last of the champagne when we woke again.

"Please," Leila said. "Do it to me again."

"You don't have to ask twice," I said.

She was already drawing me into her.

"This is too much fun," I said later.

"Don't worry about it," Leila said. "Think of it as part of the job."

I raised my eyebrows. "Do you?"

She smiled. "If I did, if I were just performing, I wouldn't have asked for an encore."

She rested her hand on my bare thigh. "No, I just thought we should enjoy what we have while we have it. I wouldn't feel guilty about it. We are a sheikh and his wife, are we not? Why shouldn't we do what we have done? It serves our job, and if you and I should have some pleasure, too, well, that is all the better. If somebody is keeping an eye on us, then they can report that the sheikh and his wife take great pleasure in each other."

"And what if nobody's keeping an eye on us?"

Leila laughed. "Then they don't know what they are missing," she said.

I laughed too.

She was right. We learned that later. Someone was keeping an eye on us. And they weren't laughing.

Chapter 9

Five days passed.

By day we tooled around the city in the big Rolls. We dined at Rules and Mirabella and Le Coq d'Or and some of the newer, trendier places that are always springing up in London. Leila shopped at Harrods and in Burlington Arcade and along Bond Street. Photographers popped up everywhere she went. Each time she poked one of her long, sleek legs out of the gleaming black door held open for her by the obliging Minoru, a photographer seemed to leap out of nowhere to snap his shutter. Leila always greeted this attention with a wide smile. The tabloids were having a field day with her.

We set aside one room in our suite for the things she bought at places like Burberry's and Fortnum & Mason, Loewe's, and the House of Floris.

By night we attended the theater and began to frequent the gambling clubs.

From time to time I received a note from some businessman interested in oil.

I met with them but left each of them thinking that the oil had been committed, that I was remaining in London only to iron out a few last-minute details. If they had any resentments, I was not aware of them.

Leila absented herself on these occasions. She and Minoru would go off to some new store she had discovered—Liberty's, Goode's, W. Bill. The pile of boxes grew higher.

"Well, I've got to do something with my time," she said. "And I figure this is what a sheikh's wife would do."

I threw up my hands in futility.

She put her arms around me and brought her mouth close to my ear. "It's fun, Nicholas," she said. "I may never have an assignment like this again. It's such fun."

Later, I was to be glad for her.

On the sixth night, shunning my Western suits, I donned my Arab raiment and went off to gamble at Madlock's, one of the more distinguished old Mayfair clubs.

AXE had set up ten thousand pounds credit there for the sheikh.

Leila dressed herself in an apple-green gown slashed from neck to navel and ankle to thigh. I sent word down for Minoru and the Rolls to be waiting.

"Your destination?" he said.

"Madlock's," I told him.

Minoru bowed and drew his breath between his teeth. I scarcely noticed the hissing sound.

It was a place of deep leather armchairs, softly lighted rooms, the mingled smells of perfume, brandy, and cigars, the clack of chips and the click of dice, roulette wheels and fresh cards.

A dapper young man met us at the door. He conducted his business well. "Your Highness," he said.

I did not reckon that he knew me from any other Arab who might have presented himself at the door. But Leila was unmistakable anywhere.

"Your pleasure, sir?" he asked.

I fixed him with my best desert-hawk gaze. "Poker."

"Splendid," he said.

"There are some gentlemen in the Green Room who will surely be delighted to have you join them. One-thousand-pound limit?"

The part of me that was Nick Carter, government employee, blanched. The sheikh merely nodded curtly. A mere pittance.

And so, with the young man leading the way, Leila and I were ushered into the Green Room and introduced to the four men seated around the table.

"Sir Hugh Benton," he said. "Michael Hyde-Arden. Dino Dominielli. Floyd Gillman."

I nodded at each of them in turn. Sir Hugh was British nobility, descended from one of those families that had been in solid with royalty since not long after the Norman conquest. The Bentons had had large holdings of land since late in the eleventh century, and when the industrial revolution came, they had managed to be in on the ground floor there, too. Sir Hugh did not work—unless finding new ways to dispose of his income could be called work.

Michael Hyde-Arden was considerably younger, but no less well endowed by his ancestors. He and Sir Hugh were a natural pair to be found together at the same table.

As for Dino Dominielli, he had started life as a garage mechanic. As a teenager he began racing motorcycles. Just before World War II, he managed to establish himself as a daring and colorful Grand Prix racer. When the war ended, he was over the hill as a competitor in road races, but not in business. He made a fortune selling home appliances in Italy.

As for Floyd Gillman, his face had peered out at the world from the cover of *Time*—one of those men, like Dominielli, who had started out with nothing and wound up with a fortune. His was a fast-food chain. Hamburgers. And they were awful.

Despite the stakes, the game proceeded in desultory fashion for the first few hours. Draw poker and five-card stud were all they played. Sir Hugh and Hyde-Arden played an expert game, pressing advantages boldly to wring out maximum profit.

Dominielli played with dash and wit, his game designed to force out would-be bluffers and the faint of heart. I suspected there was something of his old racing style in his game. He had been a chance taker, a crowd pleaser.

As for Gillman, a florid-faced man with a damp forehead and a propensity for greeting his cards with obscenities, he played like a fool. He tended to stay in too long, to run risks that showed no awareness of the odds against him. When he lost, which was frequently, he would deliver some drawling curse, mop his brow with a handkerchief plucked from the breast pocket of his dark silk suit, and snarl, "Deal 'em."

Leila stood patiently behind me, sipping champagne from a long-stemmed glass constantly replenished by liveried servants who circulated through the paneled gaming rooms.

It was precisely midnight—I remember looking at my watch—when the atmosphere of our game became suddenly charged with excitement. Looking up, I could see in the doorway the young man who had ushered me into the game.

Standing beside him—dwarfing him, actually—was one of the most enormous creatures I had ever laid eyes upon. His head, crowned with a luxuriant black topknot, nearly touched the upper frame of the door. His body, bulging with flesh and with muscle that was discernible despite the black kimono that draped him, must have weighed close to four hundred pounds. The eyes staring out of his impassive face were alert and fiery. He was Japanese—and the impression created by his topknot, his robe, and the huge proportions of his body was half-samurai, half-sumo wrestler.

"Gentlemen," the young man said, "may I introduce to you—and ask you to extend the hospitality of your table to—Mr. Sasuke Takatani."

"Certainly," Sir Hugh and Hyde-Arden said almost at once.

"Si," said Dominielli.

I nodded.

"Why not?" Gillman said. "It's already a goddamn league of nations here." He cackled at his own jest.

Sasuke Takatani nodded briefly in acknowledgement and moved to a chair one of the liveried servants placed at the table, across from me.

When he moved away from the door, I saw the girl.

She was slim and blonde, nearly as tall as Leila, with pale gray eyes and thin red lips. A black gown set off her white skin. Rubies blazed at her ears and throat. She took up a position behind Sasuke Takatani and glared over my head at Leila. When a servant brought her champagne, she tossed it down hurriedly and held out her glass for more.

A set of plaques in varying denominations was placed in front of the Japanese, and play resumed.

It did not take long to discern his style. Of all those at the table, he was the most conservative. He backed only winning cards. Otherwise, he folded his hand. Winning or losing, his expression was unchanging. His eyes, which missed nothing, betrayed no emotion. It was clear to everyone at the table that when Sasuke Takatani bet, he bet because he expected to win. And invariably he did.

At one point, Leila left the room briefly. A moment later, the blonde girl followed her. The two returned together and took up the stations they had held before.

By 3:00 A.M. Sasuke Takatani was clearly a winner. Judging by the pile of plaques in front of him, I estimated his profits at five thousand pounds. My own condition was all that I could hope for—my stake was intact. No one could accuse me of being foolhardy with AXE's money. On the other hand, there would be no arguments about the ownership of any profits.

Dominielli, was about ten thousand pounds to the good, I guessed. Sir Hugh and Hyde-Arden were up about five thousand pounds each. The source of their profits was, of course, Gillman. And he was not especially happy about it.

By now, his shirt was soaked through with perspiration. A bit of tobacco from the Havana cigars he favored was stuck to a corner of his mouth. His recourse to the constantly replenished tumbler of bourbon at his side had become more frequent. And the curses and obscenities that he had, for the most part, been mumbling all night, had become less guarded.

Sir Hugh yawned and looked at the gold watch he drew from the brocaded silken waistcoat he wore under his dinner jacket. "Gentlemen," he said, "I am sure that none of you will object if we begin to think about concluding our sport for the evening."

"Hear, hear," Hyde-Arden said.

There was a murmur of assent that stopped at Gillman.

"Goddamn!" he exclaimed. "You gonna run off and leave me sucking hind tit?"

Sir Hugh reached over to him and patted his sleeve.

"Look here, old boy," he began.

But Gillman was having none of it.

"Sheeit," he said. "Where I come from you give a man a chance to get himself even."

Hyde-Arden looked down his nose at Gillman. "I'm sure no one here objects to that. What are you out, old boy?"

Gillman riffled through his plaques, red-faced. "I figure twenty five thousand pounds."

Splendid," Hyde-Arden said. "I propose one hand, winner take all—twenty five thousand pounds. Side bets permitted, without limit. Fair enough, Mr. Gillman?"

Gillman nodded sulkily.

"All in, gentlemen?" Sir Hugh asked.

"If you will forgive me," I said. "I play for sport, not for profit. And since I show neither a profit nor a loss for the evening and have not contributed to Mr. Gillman's deficit, I would prefer to bypass this settling of accounts—if you all agree. Otherwise, with all good will, I shall take part."

There was no objection from anyone.

"Suit yourself," Gillman snarled.

The game was five-card stud. Sir Hugh began dealing. When he finished, Gillman was sitting behind a pair of jacks and a pair of sevens.

"Side bets?" Sir Hugh announced.

Gillman looked across at Sasuke Takatani. The huge Japanese was sitting like a mountain behind four hearts in sequence.

"Fifty thousand pounds," Gillman said.

"See and raise one hundred fifty thousand," said Sasuke Takatani.

There was utter silence in the room.

Gillman's voice was pinched. He pounded his fist on the table in frustration. "Goddammit to hell," he whimpered.

So the Japanese had the straight flush.

"You take my marker?" Gillman said.

"No," replied the Japanese. "I play for cash. As you say in America, cash on the barrelhead."

With that last word, I thought I saw his eyes flicker toward me for an instant.

"You gonna bust my nuts," Gillman said. "I ain't got that much cash."

"Then fold your hand, old boy," Sir Hugh said. "And we can all go home."

Gillman's face turned as gray as one of his hamburgers. His voice broke in a sob. "Busted on a goddamn full house by a Jap," he said. "Oh, goddamn. Goddamn!"

His hand was flashing across the table. "Wanna see that goddamn flush," he was saying.

Sasuke Takatani's huge ham of a hand, amazingly swift, closed over Gillman's wrist. A few cards fluttered off the table. I heard bone snap.

Gillman slumped to his knees.

"So sorry, gentlemen," Sasuke Takatani said. "Profound apologies."

"No fault of yours, old boy," Sir Hugh said, rising.

"No, indeed," said Hyde-Arden, extending his hand to the Japanese. He gestured with his free hand toward Gillman, who had regained his feet and was staggering out of the room, clutching his fractured wrist. "Bit of a bad show there, I'm afraid."

Dominielli waved his hand in an airy farewell. "A pleasure, gentlemen," he said in his deep, mellifluous voice. "Until the next time."

In the excitement, no one but me had noticed the cards lying on the floor—Sasuke Takatani's hand. His hole card was the deuce of spades. There had been no flush after all. For the first and only time all evening—when the stakes were highest—Sasuke Takatani had bluffed.

I pretended to have seen nothing. I dipped my head in silent farewell as the players left the room, until only Leila and I and the Japanese and the blonde girl remained.

I nodded toward him and turned to go.

"One moment, please," he said.

"Yes?" I said.

"Perhaps this is not the time or place," he said in the smooth, cultured voice that did not seem to match the warrior-wrestler image of his hair, clothing, and body, "but I understand that you are in the business of selling oil."

"You are correct," I said.

"You will not be offended if I raise the subject here?"

"I am a businessman," I said. "If you wish to talk here, I am not averse to the idea."

"I would like to bid on your oil," he said.

"I appreciate your interest, but I am afraid it is already spoken for."

"A pity," he said, gripping my arm. His fingers felt like lead weights against my biceps.

"Yes," I said, "a pity."

His fingers continued to hold me.

"But there is always the future," he persisted softly.

"Let me be frank with you," I said. "I am sure you are a man who appreciates a straight approach." I thought of the little ploy that had done in the burger baron. "The interests controlling the reserves of oil I have been empowered to commit are desirous of a long-term arrangement. And that is what I came here to negotiate for them. Only a few minor details remain to be worked out."

The huge Takatani frame heaved with a sigh.

"Long-term commitments in an unstable world." He shook his head sadly. "Most dangerous," he said with a hint of menace. "One must seek to learn from history, not to insult it. Perhaps the interests you represent would be willing to reconsider.''

"I tend to doubt it," I told him.

"One never knows," he said. "There are inducements.''

"At this point, they seem to be more than satisfied with the arrangements I have been making for them.''

Sasuke Takatani released his grip and patted my arm. Each pat seemed like a punch. He smiled at me. "Forgive me, I press you," he said. "I make you uncomfortable. Most impolite. Perhaps you take offense. But I assure you, no offense is meant. We are two civilized men, and there is no reason why we cannot talk. Perhaps, as I said, this is not the time or place for us to discuss business. Perhaps in another place at another time, you and I can profitably exchange our views.''

"Yes, that may be so," I said.

He gave my arm another of his devastating pats.

"I will tell you what," he said. "Come pay me a visit tomorrow at my place in the country. Tell your man to bring you to Dragon House in Oxfordshire. Everyone knows it. We can at least enjoy the glorious British countryside. We can talk. And—who knows?—we may even transact some business. What do you say?''

He carried it off with a good deal of charm.

"Very well," I said. "Tomorrow.''

He leaned close to my ear. "Bring your lady, if you wish," he said. "I am sure she will find much to amuse her. Or, if you prefer to leave her behind, that is well, too. The women can sometimes be a burden.''

I nodded.

"Come at about noon. We will stroll a little. We shall have a light lunch and talk, and by nightfall, you will be back in London again."

"Very well," I said. "Noon tomorrow."

I turned to Leila. She and the blonde girl were exchanging cool glances.

"Come, Leila," I said.

"Yes, my sheikh," she said. I thought I caught a certain stress on the *my*.

Madlock's was closing down for the night. A few of the rooms would be open until dawn. But in others the tables had fallen silent and lay covered under white dust cloths.

The cool night air outside tasted good. I drew it deeply into my lungs, enjoying the freshness, until Minoru drew the Rolls up in front of us.

Leila put the back of her hand to her brow. "Oh," she said, "that champagne!"

"Have sip of sherry," said Minoru, holding the door open and beckoning her inside the car. "Best thing. You be surprised. Make you feel much better."

I poured a little for her into one of the crystal glasses, and she sipped it while we returned to our hotel.

Minoru bowed us out of the car.

"You feel better?" he asked.

"Why, yes," Leila said. "Thank you, Minoru."

The Japanese bared his teeth in his customary smile. "Good night, lady." he said.

"Good night, Minoru, and thank you."

"You want car tomorrow?" he asked.

"Yes," I said. "In the morning, about ten. We're going to Oxfordshire. A place called Dragon House."

"Very good," Minoru said. "I be waiting when you ready."

By the time we reached our room, Leila had grown very sleepy. I had to help her into bed.

"Do lovely things to my body," she said.

I began moving my lips over her breasts.

"She hates him, you know," Leila murmured.

"Who?"

"The blonde girl—Fleur. She hates the Japanese."

"Why?"

"I'm not quite sure," Leila said in a far-off voice. "He won her in a poker game. From a German. She's French, she says. Now all she says is 'Japan *kaput*.' "

"Interesting," I said, spreading Leila's thighs.

"Ah," she said. "Ah!"

I should have been asking more questions. I should have been paying more attention. Instead, I was luxuriating in Leila's receptive body.

Just the way it had been planned.

Chapter 10

"Go without me," Leila said the next morning. She lay in bed, one bare arm shielding her eyes from the sunlight. "I'm sorry. It's very unprofessional of me, I know. But that champagne . . . I don't think I could stand up. My head, my mouth." She groaned.

"Do you want me to get a doctor?" I asked.

"No. I just want to sleep. Perhaps later I'll feel better. Who knows?" Her voice was listless.

Just a bad hangover, I thought as I dressed in my robes.

"Could you close the drapes?" she asked. "The light hurts my eyes."

When I was ready to leave, I sat on the edge of the bed. "Are you sure you'll be all right?" I said.

With an effort, she smiled.

"Don't worry," she said. And then she frowned. "I should be going with you," she said. "That's my job. That's what I'm supposed to do."

She struggled to raise herself. Gently, I pushed her back down on the bed.

"Don't worry about it," I said. "I'll be all right."

"Yes," she said weakly. "I suppose so. I suppose so."

"I've got to go now," I said.

She put her arms around me, and her eyes opened wide.

"Be careful," she said.

I rose to leave. "Don't worry. Get some sleep. You'll feel better when you wake up. I'll be back this evening. We'll have dinner and go dancing."

"Yes," she said. Her eyes were closed again. Her voice seemed to be growing weaker. "That sounds nice. But I must remember."

"Remember what?" I asked, standing by the door.

I could barely hear her answer. "That champagne," she said. "Must avoid the champagne. It's dangerous; it's danger—"

There were two chauffeurs waiting for me outside the hotel. One of them was Minoru, and he was looking uncomfortable. He bowed as I approached him.

"Some sort of mixup," he said. "Gentleman from Oxfordshire send car to bring you to his home. Minoru also bring car to take you to Oxfordshire. Two cars. Only one person." He giggled in embarrassment. "What you wish do?"

"I shall go in the other car," I told him.

"Lady not come, eh?"

"No," I said. "So why don't you wait here. Perhaps later she will need you."

Minoru bowed again. "Yes. I wait. You go. So sorry lady not come. So sorry."

The other chauffeur was Japanese too. His black cap

sat squarely on his close-cropped hair. His face was lean. Above his high cheekbones, his eyes smoldered like dark coals. He stood at attention beside the door of his Daimler Limousine until I moved toward it, and then, with swift, precise movements that wasted not a single bit of energy, he reached out with his black-gloved hand, opened the door, bowed me inside, closed the door, and eased into the driver's seat.

The stately automobile glided away from the curb and flowed smoothly into the busy stream of London traffic. I settled back into the leather seats.

In a short time, the city had fallen behind us. The huge car sped over narrow roads that wound between green fields.

The driver said nothing. His hands, encased in gleaming black leather, never left their 10 a.m.-2 p.m. position on the steering wheel. His neck remained rigid under its dark bristle of hair. But once, as he gazed into the rear-view mirror, his eyes met mine. The mirror caught a bit of his mouth, too—enough for me to catch the smile of amused contempt. He knew I had seen him, and he didn't care.

My pulse raced momentarily. I resisted the impulse to check my weapons. All my senses were quickening. In my mind's eye, there was a momentary vision of Leila, sleep tousled, her arms about me, her eyes wide. "Be careful," I could hear her saying again.

And then, up ahead, I could see the wrought-iron skeleton that was the enormous gate to the estate. Twin black dragons, breathing metal fire as though to incinerate the unwary interloper, reclined at its summit. And beyond, through the vertical ribbing, I could see a broad expanse of immaculate green lawn, the obedient martial symmetry of its grassy blades disrupted only by the pearl ribbon of driveway that bisected it like a sash while drawing the eye up a rise carefully laid out to conceal the grounds beyond from the casual passerby.

As the Daimler grew close to the gate, the black-gloved hand of the chauffeur touched a switch on the knurled-wood dashboard. The huge iron barrier, responding to some electronic signal, eased majestically open, and the limousine, with no slackening of speed, rolled with equal majesty onto the domain of Sasuke Tokatani.

At the top of the rise, just as some eighteenth-century architect had planned, Dragon House burst upon the eye and seized the breath: a great panorama of lawn, a central lane of sculptured shrubbery, the great, sprawling, winged manor house in faded yellow under the broad blue ocean of sky that played host to a flotilla of white clouds. To either side and beyond, a cool green forest. It was an orchestration of history, wealth, and most of all, entrenched and crushing power.

In the distance, as the car across the half mile of unblemished gravel leading to Dragon House, I could see a squad of men, clad in white coveralls, finish calisthenics and, with practiced order, form themselves into a line of joggers who vanished quickly into the forest like so much white spume consumed in a dark green sea.

When the Daimler drew to a halt at the foot of the broad steps—flanked by sculptured, reclining dragons—leading to the main entrance, the chauffeur glided out and held open the limousine door for me.

At the top of the stairway stood a frail old man with a thin wisp of pale gray beard barely covering his bony chin. He wore a black kimono. And when I looked up at him, he bowed deeply and took three steps backward, beckoning me upward. As I drew near him, he turned and led the way toward the massive oaken doors of the manor house. In the sunlight, the brass knocker and bulbous doorknob gleamed blindingly.

The old man's frail hand reached out. His body tensed slightly, and with surprising ease for one who seemed so withered and twiglike as to be prey for even a vagrant breeze, he swung open the door.

I could see several things at once. A bit of wall, where hung a pair of samurai swords and crossed Arisaka rifles—the kind Japanese troops carried in World War II. And I could see the woman called Fleur.

"Welcome," she said. "Welcome to Dragon House. Mr. Takatani is occupied at present and was very much concerned that you might interpret has failure to be here to greet you himself as a slight. He has no wish to offend you, Your Highness. And so as a token of his good will, he asked me to appear in his place for a little while and to attend to your wishes and needs. Is there anything I might offer you? Some refreshments, perhaps?"

"No," I said a bit distractedly, as my eyes roved over the grandeur of the manor house.

Fleur's small white teeth appeared behind her pale lips in a cool smile.

"It is very impressive, is it not? Mr. Takatani has highly developed tastes. Only the best pleases him."

The slight but extraordinary emphasis she placed on

the word *best* left no doubt that Fleur included herself among the treasures of the household. In the relative dimness of the great entrance hall leading to another broad expanse of stairway, amid the dark luster of rich paneling and the expected array of armor, there were—carefully integrated—awesome expressions of later and earlier artistry: paintings and sculptures the world's foremost museums would have fought over; small cabinets of delicate Chinese porcelains and of Etruscan gold. Ancient jewels shimmered against green baize.

Only the two cheap-looking 6.5-mm type-38 rifles (known as Arisakas, in honor of the nineteenth-century army colonel who headed the Tokyo Arsenal and developed the original version, first produced in 1897) seemed incongruous. Even had the only two items in the entrance hall been the two samurai swords crossed above them, the effect would have been striking. The swords were clearly the work of master craftsmen and were of inestimable value. But the rifles . . . I must have been staring at them. Fleur hastened to interrupt my train of thought.

"The house is most impressive, is it not?" she said. "Fifty-six rooms in all. Built originally for a Duke. Mr. Takatani took possession of it last year. Then everything was redecorated to his taste. Everything is of the best."

Once again that slight but extraordinary emphasis on the word drew attention, not to the immense wealth apparent just in the entrance hallway, but to Fleur. I could not help glancing at her, as she must have known

I would. At that moment, she turned, so that the light filtering through a stained-glass window above the stairway streamed through her loose-fitting gray gown.

It was obvious she was wearing nothing beneath it. Quite clearly visible were a tuft of pale pubic hair and the firm cones of her breasts.

Fleur pretended not to be aware of the effect. "Perhaps I might show you some of the other rooms," she said, extending her hand.

It was impossible not to accept her invitation. I reached out and took her cool hand. Her tapering fingers closed about mine, but not before fumbling slightly, enabling her nails to gently rake my palm.

"Did I hurt you?" she said innocently.

Before I could respond, she had bent her head and pressed her lips lingeringly against my palm. For an instant, her tongue pulsed against the flesh.

"It must feel better now," she said. "Come. I will show you around."

And so began the guided tour, along hallways ablaze with the work of old masters—Rembrandts, Reubenses, Titians glowed from the paneling. Then into rooms decorated with the work of newer masters—whole salons filled with Renoirs, Monets, Manets, Picassos. Nooks and crannies filled with sculpture by Brancusi and mobiles, sketches, and circuses by Calder. A cabinet filled with Greek vases. A showcase like a miniature universe with diamonds in place of stars.

Yet so extensive was the manor house that it was possible to feel no clash of periods in the display of treasures. For the onlooker, though, there was a sense of being dashed forward and backward in time and churned among differing estimates of artistry.

Fleur clung to my hand, keeping generally a step or so ahead of me as she described the various treasures, occasionally falling back a pace and halting in front of some painting that called for more than a word or two. At times during these pauses, seemingly without premeditation but too often to be without design, I could feel her thigh against mine, the flesh seeming to speak hotly to my flesh, while her tongue spoke impersonally to my ears.

The cumulative effect was remarkable—an impression of the enormous wealth of Sasuke Takatani and the power that lay behind the wealth. And more immediately, the aura of calculated eroticism that surrounded the woman called Fleur.

At the end of a long hallway, she halted in front of an ornate medieval tapestry depicting a fair-haired maiden kneeling above the lance-pierced body of a fallen knight.

"I first saw this as a small child—in a book. A picture of it, I mean. I could not read. I could only imagine. She loved him, of course, and he died." Her fingers reached out and stopped just before touching the trickle of blood that ran from his side. "I wondered what happened to her afterward. Who took care of her?"

She started to say something else but caught herself as though on the verge of violating her responsibilities as a hostess.

"I'm sorry," she said. Once again I felt her thigh

against mine. She turned and faced me. Her cool gray eyes—eyes that matched the color of her gown—met mine. "Do you keep secrets?" she said.

"Yes?" I said.

Her eyes calculated. And then, having made her decision, she reached behind the floor-to-ceiling tapestry and touched something concealed in the wood paneling. I could hear what must have been a section of wall sliding open, followed by a hint of cool, damp air.

"Quickly," Fleur said.

Tugging my hand, she led me behind the tapestry, though a section of wall that had indeed slid open, and into utter darkness. For an instant, Fleur abandoned my hand. I was tempted to reach for the deadly knife hidden under the folds of my robe. But I sensed no danger. There was the scrape of a match, and a candle flared into life. And then another and another.

Compared to some of the other rooms of Dragon House, the room was small. But by any ordinary standard, it was more than spacious. Landscape portraits of green fields and quiet streams overhung with great leafy trees lent it a peaceful quality. Thick green carpeting added to the effect. The only furniture was a wide bed.

Fleur finished lighting the candles, extinguished the match, and tossed it into the inevitable fireplace before turning to face me. There was a mischievous smile on her lips.

"Pleasant, is it not?" she said. "No one knows of it but me."

"Most attractive," I told her.

"I discovered it quite by accident. I suspect one of

the dukes had it constructed for pleasures he hoped to conceal from his wife.'' She emitted a humorless chuckle. ''Men are like that.''

Her gray gown whispering in the still air, her pale lips warmed by the flickering candlelight, Fleur glided softly across the distance that separated us, until there was no distance at all. She pressed her body against me, and then her lips. Her tongue explored my mouth.

She withdrew it and pulled me toward the bed, sitting me at its edge while she remained standing.

''I want you to take me away with you,'' she said.

Her hands reached up and unclasped the diamond pin that fastened her gown at the shoulder.

''Why?''

The pin was opened.

''There is no future for me here.''

''No future?'' I gestured to encompass the house, the grounds, all the obvious wealth.

Holding her gown together, Fleur gestured for me to recline on the bed.

When I had made myself comfortable, she undraped the gown. Her pale body, with its delicate pink-tipped breasts and pale hair, was more voluptuous than I had suspected. I started to reach for her.

''Be patient,'' she said, sliding into the bed beside me. One hand reached behind my neck and drew me to her mouth. The other, practiced and sure, found its way beneath my robes to begin a own slow, rhythmic dialogue of flesh.

Fleur withdrew her mouth from mine. I reached out to pull her toward me again. She placed a finger over my lips.

"Patience," she counseled, while the other conversation continued. "Patience while I tell you a story. And then you shall enjoy the best of happy endings." Again that special emphasis on the word *best*.

"Unlike you, my sheikh," she began, "I have had to make my way in the world since my earliest childhood. My first recollections of life are of an orphanage. A very special orphanage, where all the children were the children of French women raped by Nazi soldiers. And rejected by their mothers.

"French citizens, yes. But the bastards of Europe. Beyond the bare necessities of life, we received nothing, except the right to be used by others. At the age of six, I was placed in the employ of a farmer, for which the orphanage received a fee. My days began just before dawn and ended just before midnight. I cleaned his house. I tended his animals. I worked beside him in the fields. He had a wife who did nothing except cook his meals. When I was eight, she told me I would take over the cooking, too.

"When I displeased them, I was beaten. And despite my best efforts, I seemed to displease them often, because beating me was their only form of recreation. Once a month, one of the officials of the orphanage would come to the house to collect the fee. On those occasions, I was beaten in advance and told to be on my best behavior. It made no difference. The orphanage was not interested in me, only in its fee. The officials never spared me more than a glance.

"When they received their money, they would look at me and thunder: 'Be obedient. You should be grateful to these people for taking you into their home.'

"And so the years went by. A routine broken only when I outgrew my clothing and the farmer's wife brought me some fresh rags from who knows where. A routine broken only by the visits from the orphanage officials and the injunction to be obedient and grateful.

"When I was twelve, the farmer's wife died.

"Two nights later, as I was preparing for bed in my room in the attic, the farmer opened my door.

" 'My woman is dead,' he said. 'You are old enough to do more.' He shut the door behind him and raped me.

"I ran away the next morning, an uneducated girl without a friend in the world. I do not wish to bore you. I was taken to Paris by an Algerian truck driver who received a modest sum for me when he sold me to a cousin who operated a brothel. He handed back a few francs, took me upstairs, and raped me."

"I spent the next three years there. I was befriended by a woman named Annette. 'You are beautiful, you know,' she said. 'And you are a woman now. You can make your way in the world.'

"She arranged for me the acquisition of false papers, and she too received a modest sum—although significantly larger than the truck driver's—for spiriting me into the custody of a German business executive.

"His name was Dieter. I am sure you would recognize the rest of his name. Perhaps you would even know him. His family has been associated with German heavy industry for six generations. One of those aristocratic German marriages tinged with depravity. His wife preferred women and inflicting pain. She went her way. Dieter went his. With people like these, the marriages survive too. Appearances are all. Dieter kept me in a small apartment on the grounds of his factory. There was no reason for him to be kind, but he was.

" 'Life is strange, Fleur,' he said one day after we had made love. 'I will not live forever, and I have been thinking about your future. I suppose I could give you money. But I have seen money turn worthless overnight. I could give you property. But in my lifetime I have seen property destroyed. So I have decided to give you something that you will possess all your life, something that, if used wisely, will gain you money and property should you so wish. In any case, it will enable you to fend for yourself, no matter what.'

"My education began shortly after that. A series of tutors began to visit me. I was educated as Dieter had been—privately, in languages and art and history and philosophy. The social amenities that had been no part of my farmhouse and brothel life were instilled in me.

"I discovered that I was starved for knowledge. I was a surprisingly apt pupil. In four years, by the time I was nineteen, Dieter told me that I was the equal of any woman he had ever met.

" 'Between what you have learned here and what you learned in that brothel,' he said, 'you are truly a formidable creature.'

"Three days later, he was dead, the victim of a massive heart attack.

"I could not attend the funeral. I was, after all, only his mistress. The German newspapers showed pictures of his wife in her black dress and black veil weeping over his bier.

"I suppose I should have left then. Immediately. It's

easy enough to say that now. But the truth was that I had never been on my own. All my life I had been in the custody of others—the orphanage, the farmer, the brothel, Dieter. For all the education he had given me, I still thought of myself as a whore. Besides, all I had was a few marks. Dieter had given me a generous allowance, but I had saved nothing.''

"On the night after the funeral, there was a knock at my door. When I opened it, I was confronted by the plant manager.

" 'Now that Dieter is dead,' he said, 'I suppose you are mine. He pushed me against the wall, tore away my clothing, and raped me.'

" 'Good, eh?' he said when he was finished.

"When I did not respond, he blackened my eye.

"His name was Ernst. All he shared with Dieter was a yearning for the good things of life. Of taste, of manners, of knowledge, he possessed none. He was coarse. A manager. One of thousands. But he had spent his life envying Dieter. And now he thought he was Dieter. But he lacked two things—the breeding and the money. He was given to gambling, and before long he was heavily in debt. One night he emerged from a gaming room in an after-hours club in Frankfurt. He was accompanied by a huge Japanese. 'You are his now,' Ernest said. And that night I became the possession of Takatani. Two days later, Ernest was found dead. That was three years ago. I have traveled with Mr. Takatani and lived with him ever since. And now I must move on.''

"Why?" I asked.

"It is something I sense," she said. "Something I

learned from Dieter. Some awareness of the tides of history that thrust first one country and then another into a position of dominance and then recede and bring forth new powers. Perhaps it was bred into me out of rape and subjugation. Perhaps I learned it being sold in one way or another. I don't know. But this much I feel: It is time for me to leave Takatani. I do not know him. He is a strange man. All that interests him about me is what I can do for him in bed. I know nothing of his business or the people who surround him, except for the old man. Do you remember the old man? The one who met you at the door?"

"Yes," I said.

"You have seen him before," Fleur told me.

I started to say no, but Fleur placed one cool finger on my lips.

"A year ago," she said, "his picture was in every newspaper in the world. The old man of the islands, they called him."

And then I remembered. Nearly a full generation after the end of World War II, he had emerged from the jungles of one of the Pacific islands in response to an appeal that invoked the name of Emperor Hirohito, and he had surrendered. His uniform was still in good repair. He still carried his Arisaka rifle—two, in fact. He was decently nourished and ready to fight, he said. For a couple of months, doctors marveled at him. Newspapers fussed over him. And then he became yesterday's hero.

"You mean that's him?" I said.

"Yes. He is the only one who speaks to me. He managed to learn some English from discarded books and newspapers he found while hiding. 'Everyone forgot me,' he told me one day. 'Despite what I had done for Japan, there was no work, no money. I was better off on the island. I did not understand the new Japan and its foreign ways. And then when I was full of despair, Sasuke Takatani came to me and begged that I join him. We are the new samurai, he told me.' "

It was Nick Carter and not the sheikh who said to Fleur, "Interesting. What do you suppose he meant by that?"

"I don't know. He never spoke of it again. Most of the time, he busies himself with his duties as Takatani's personal servant."

Fleur's practiced hand was still carrying on its rhythmic conversation beneath my robes.

"You must take me away from here," she said softly. "Take me, take me, take me. Perhaps you yourself do not want me. I have seen your woman. Perhaps I would be trouble. But perhaps you have a friend. Someone such as yourself. An Arab. Japan is finished. I cannot linger here much longer."

She guided me to her.

"You see," she said in a caressing whisper. "The tides of history are changing. If my life has taught me anything, it is to obey them."

Her body undulated beneath me.

"Surely," she said, as her legs locked about my back and her muscles closed with practiced artistry and she began to drain me as never before, "surely, surely there is someone who appreciates . . . the best."

Chapter 11

Clad in black, his inky hair pulled back in the classic *chomage*—the topknot of the ancient samurai—Sasuke Takatani glowered at me from behind his desk.

Beneath my robes my loins still basked in the moist warmth of Fleur, and her scent lingered in my nostrils so clearly that I could not believe that Takatani could fail to know everything that had happened.

The old man—in my mind I called him simply "the Survivor"—finished laying out the tea things, bowed, and backed from the immense paneled room.

Far off, through the window behind my host, I could see the white-coveralled men emerging from the forest, double-timing easily over the soft green turf until they disappeared from the expanse of spotless glass through which I beheld them.

Takatani poured the tea and proffered the first cup to me. With a visible effort, he erased the anger from his visage.

"Forgive me," he said. "I am a poor host. It was not

my intention to keep you waiting. I trust that the woman has proved herself worthy in my stead.''

I gazed steadily at him. His face betrayed nothing. The poker player.

"More than worthy," I told him with an equally straight face.

She had left me only minutes before, outside the lofty doorway leading to Takatani's study. Squeezing my hand, she had said, "Please, find a way for me to go."

I was about to answer, when the Survivor swung open the doors from the inside and with a low bow beckoned me within. In her gray gown, Fleur glided from sight like a tormented wraith who had wandered, anguished, for centuries through the endless corridors of Dragon House.

Now Takatani was saying, "It pleases me that she has found favor with you. I should be more than shamed had the foreign woman been an unworthy representative of mine. As for my display of ill manners, I hope you will excuse that, too."

I hastened to assure Takatani that I was in no way offended, that I was delighted with the opportunity to tour his house and overwhelmed with his taste.

At this, he permitted himself a small smile. "You are a man who appreciates the good things of life," he said. "Come, let us finish our tea, and we shall walk a bit and talk."

He drained his tiny cup and raised his huge bulk from his chair. The Survivor appeared silently and whisked away the tray, then reappeared to open the front doors for us. I could appreciate why he had eluded capture for so long in the Pacific jungles. Takatani and I began to stroll along the immaculate lawn and around one wing of the house, toward the forest.

"Your visit is most timely," he said. "The news this morning has been no less than distressing. I have been endeavoring to obtain commitments of oil. Endeavoring without sufficient success. And this fills me with fear."

His words were so strong that I looked at him quizzically.

"Japan cannot survive without oil," he said. "What do you know of the history of Japan?"

"Not a great deal, I must confess."

"A most remarkable nation," Takatani said. "Marked by destiny for greatness. Protected by the *kamikaze*—the 'Divine Wind'—from Mongol invasion on August 14, 1281. Blessed with the samurai, faithful to their leaders, indifferent to physical hardship. Isolated for centuries from the outside world. A fertile soil for the ideal of *bushido*—selfless devotion to the arts of war marked by a willingness to die. A nation of scholarship, never too proud to learn; a nation where, in time, the technology of the outside world was assimilated, mastered, and improved upon.

"And when the old feudal ways were suppressed in the nineteenth century, it was a nation ready to produce the *zaibatsu*—the great industrial combines. And so it moved into the twentieth century and toward the realization of a destiny that lay beyond its island boundaries. For Japan is a nation blessed in many ways, but it is not a nation blessed with natural wealth.

"Thus began the adventures that ended in the rubble

117

of Hiroshima and Nagasaki. As for myself, I have little recollection of a time before then. In fact, I do not know who I am. My earliest memory is of foraging for food in the embers of a house in Tokyo. In those years, I was forever hungry. Not long afterward, the Americans came. I did errands for them. I found them women. They patted my head. They tossed me money. They gave me candy. And sometimes when I brought them women, they gave me nothing. Sometimes they abused the women.

"In time, I grew to loathe the Americans and to hate what they had done to my country and to my people. I do not know precisely how old I am. But by the time I was about ten I was a whoremaster, a black marketeer, and deeply involved with the *yakuza*—the professional-criminal class.

"I did not think of myself as an outlaw. I thought of myself as a samurai, in the service of my emperor. I had taken the name Sasuke Takatani, given to me by an old man I had hired to instill in me some of the ancient ways that were even then vanishing from Japan. I became adept at the martial arts. I learned the skills of sumo. I learned of my country's history. And of its perilous economic situation.

"The old man who tutored me was the product of an interesting heritage. His father was a founder of the Kokuryukai, an ultranationalist organization. It is also known as the Society of the River Amur. But it is perhaps best known as the Black Dragon Society. The old man himself had had a son who was a member of an organization of similar aims. It flourished briefly in the early thirties, when it was composed of young men of great nationalistic pride. It was known as the League of Blood. The boy was killed in the war. And figuratively speaking, I became the old man's son. So perhaps it is inevitable that I should have fallen heir to a special view of Japan and its destiny.

"Perhaps what I tell you has repelled you. But the Arab people have also known humiliation and subjugation at the hands of outsiders, which has kept them from realizing their rightful destiny. And so, at the risk of disgusting you, I tell you of my life. You may regard me as a whoremaster and an outlaw. I regard myself as a protector of my people—the people of Japan."

There was a moment of silence before Takatani continued.

"Sometimes when Japanese say they are speaking frankly, they mean they are about to be rude. I use the phrase in its Western sense. I am being frank with you because I hope that as an Arab, as a representative of a people prevented by the exploitation of Americans and other Western nations from realizing their true destiny, you will appreciate the intensity of my feelings for my own country.

"For myself"—he gestured with his enormous hand at our surroundings—"I need nothing. Long ago, I put behind me the petty criminal operations that were the source of my wealth. Like the Mafia in the United States, I have legitimized my operations. Although I seek no personal notoriety, the interests I control qualify me as a successor to the original *zaibatsu.*

"But my interests are nothing if Japan is imperiled. Those who took my nation to war in the nineteen-thirties against China, and against the United States in the nineteen-forties, were correct in their fundamental analysis but wrong in their timing and strategy.

"Japan must expand. Japan must protect herself against a scarcity of the resources necessary to operate her great industrial complexes. The island is overpopulated. Should Japan's industry fail—fail, let us say, for want of oil—chaos would reign. I cannot permit myself to allow that to happen."

He moved across the broad expanse of even green grass in long, loose strides, his black kimono billowing behind him, his voice rumbling softly from the vast cavern of his chest. His *chomage* gleamed under the bright sun, and with the manor house behind us and only the forest ahead, it was difficult not to believe that I had been transported back in time to a feudal Japan where a man like Sasuke Takatani might have been supreme among samurai.

There was a softness to his tone that belied the intensity of his emotions when he spoke of his vision of himself and his country. There was no doubting his sincerity. But there are sunshine patriots, too. How far was Takatani willing to go to assure the destiny of Japan? How far had he already gone?

And where did his loyalties really lie? I had been thinking of him as a samurai. But I remember something else. The samurai had masters. Was Takatani truly a latter-day samurai? Or was he one of the *ronin*—the masterless warriors, a class that once gave Japan some of its most daring and violent adventurers?

There was something fierce and independent about him, something explosive.

Be careful, I told myself. And for a moment, just for

a moment under that bright sun as we moved across the grass, I remembered Leila. She had said the same thing.

Up ahead, just beyond the line of trees at the beginning of the forest, I could see what looked like the mouth of a cove.

"Do you like automobiles?" Takatani asked.

"Most certainly," I told him.

"I was certain you were a man who would," he said. "I like them too. They are remarkable both technologically and aesthetically, and so I have indulged myself to a certain extent when it comes to automobiles."

I could see that the entrance of what appeared to be a cave was actually a paved ramp that sloped underground.

"I think you will enjoy what you are about to see," Takatani said. "I doubt that there is anything quite like it in all the world."

And indeed, as far as I knew, there was not. Beneath the forest floor, Takatani had constructed the most enormous garage I had ever seen.

And arrayed, gleaming, along the concrete floor, was his collection. I pride myself in knowing something about automobiles. This collection was special. It ranged from A, for Abadal, produced by Francisco Abada in Madrid in 1912, to Z, for Zwickau, the first mass-produced German car with a fiberglass body.

But it was what was in between that dazzled the eye and took away the breath. If Takatani's collection of art had been impressive, there were no words to describe his automobiles.

Gleaming under the lights, I saw, were a 1904 Delaugere, a 1910 Delauney-Belleville, Hispano-Suizas, Mercers, a tiny white Austrian Daimler from 1912, an immaculate little Peugeot convertible from 1923, huge Mercedes-Benzes, Marmons, Lancias, Bentleys, Duesenbergs, Packards, Morgans, bright red Alfa Romeos, Rolls-Royces by the dozen, Bugattis, including the Royale and the type-57 Atlantique, Cisitalias, Ferraris, Aston Martins, Lagondas.

I picked out a dead white Mercedes S, the six-cylinder supercharged model that set the German record for sports cars of 110.4 miles an hour in 1928. There were a Rolls-Royce Silver Ghost double cabriolet, with body by Barker, a 1934 Duesenberg Model J Beverly sedan, a 1935 Mercedes-Benz 540K cabriolet with Sindelfingen body; a 1937 Rolls Royce P III sedan with special Mulliner coachwork. The 540K, if I remembered correctly, had been used by the Krupp munitions family. Churchill had ridden in the Rolls, as had Montgomery of Alamein and other British officers. The two cars sat side by side—an ironic juxtaposition.

Here and there along the spotless floor, I could see Japanese in white coveralls tinkering with an engine or polishing the already immaculate and gleaming paint-and metalwork.

I looked at Takatani. It was as though he had read my thoughts.

"Yes," he said, "every one of them is completely restored and in flawless working condition. Each one is kept ready to go at all times."

"They are most admirable," I said.

Takatani clapped his hands.

The white-clad workmen appeared on the run, arrayed themselves in as orderly a fashion as they had arrayed the cars, and waited at attention.

Takatani saluted them with a bow. They bowed in return. He clapped his hands once more, and like well-trained troops, they returned on the double to their positions.

It was the first time I had seen them at close range. Each, I noticed, wore a dagger at his belt. All seemed in peak condition.

"A spirited group," I said.

"Yes," Takatani agreed. "Like the automobiles. Spirited." He added enigmatically, "Like the automobiles, oil makes them run."

He had a last look at his collection. "Shall we go?"

I nodded.

We were about to leave, when I heard footsteps moving rapidly toward us from a passageway leading out of the main room.

Takatani paused. "Excuse me," he said.

Takatani bent to hear what the white-clad messenger had to tell him. Then the two marched off together. At the intersection where the passageway branched off from the main room, they entered a glassed-in office. For a moment, a light illuminated the room. I glimpsed a glass-fronted cabinet filled with racks of submachine guns. I saw Takatani pick up a telephone, listen, nod, and smile. And then, though I had pretended to be oblivious, the aide quickly lowered a black shade.

Takatani returned in a few moments. I pretended to have been absorbed the entire time in the landscape of cars.

"Sorry to have kept you waiting," he said. "But

some news from London that I had been expecting has just reached me."

"Good news, I trust," I said.

"Oh, yes," he said. "Yes, indeed. Very much so."

He rubbed his huge hands together. "Some tea? Or perhaps you prefer champagne."

Chapter 12

Once again, the great Daimler was rolling swiftly over the road between Dragon House and London. The same driver, his hands now bare, holding the polished wood of the steering wheel in the same 10-o'clock, 2-o'clock grip, peered straight ahead, except for those rare instances when he smirked at me in the rear-view mirror.

As I leaned back in the soft leather seat, I could hear Takatani's voice and the words he spoke as I took my leave of him after telling him that my oil was committed.

"You are a businessman," he said. "If by any chance your commitment is not firm, if by any chance an offer of more money will cause you to tell me that your oil is not committed, then consider that offer made. If there is any possibility at all of a reconsideration, then I urge you to reconsider. To me it is not a simple business matter. Perhaps to you. But not to me. To me, this is a matter involving the fate of 110 million Japanese."

His voice deepened, and beneath his black kimono he seemed more massive and menacing than ever. "So I urge you to think again," he said. "It is prudent to do so. As you may have noticed, I play for big stakes."

The Survivor held open the door of the Daimler while I seated myself.

Sasuke Takatani stood at the top of the stairway between the stone dragons. "Consult your principals," he said. "I shall await your call. At any time, day or night."

I looked up at him and raised my hand in a farewell salute. And as I gazed, my eye was caught by a figure in one of the manor windows above and directly behind him. It was Fleur, motionless, silent but demanding, like a mannequin in a shop window.

She was completely nude.

One more element of the puzzle that was Dragon House.

I made up my mind to wait until the next morning. I would telephone Takatani and tell him my principals had given a courteous hearing to my transmission of his entreaty and had turned it down flat, finally, and without hope of reconsideration at any time.

That would either end the matter or goad Takatani to some kind of action. In either case, I told myself, I would know within forty-eight hours whether I had been wasting my time or matching wits with someone who was exactly what he suggested himself to be—a man who would brook no obstacle to his vision of his country's destiny.

Forty-eight hours, I told myself.

I was wrong.

There was no trace of Leila when I returned to the

hotel. I called the desk. "She left here at about noon, Your Highness," I was told. "No, she left no message. She took the car. But the car came back about an hour ago. Would you like me to inquire of your chauffeur?"

"No," I said, "I'll ask him myself."

I found the car garaged beneath the hotel. There was no trace of Minoru either. At least at first.

But when I opened the trunk, I found him grinning up at me, quite dead. His head had been severed with exquisite skill. Few weapons on earth can perform such a feat. One of them is the samurai sword, wielded by an expert. The body had been folded slightly to fit the trunk. It lay in an embryonic position. Minoru still wore his black gloves—which made the third glove that lay near his corpse that much more conspicuous.

Poor Minoru. I suppose it had not been easy for him, a foreigner in a strange country. I imagined he would have leaped at the opportunity for a conversation with a fellow Japanese. And a chauffeur at that. It was too late for him now. I closed the trunk. Leila was another matter.

There was nothing I could prove, but the pieces of the puzzle were beginning to fit together, and I had a hunch they would fit even better after another visit to Dragon House. If anyone had been expecting me to sit still and wait for word of Leila, they were wrong. As far as I was concerned, there had been too much waiting. It was over now, and I could feel the excitement surging through me—an excitment mingled with renewed hatred for whoever had set off the chain of events that had put a bullet through poor Taff and had stolen Leila and had made Nick Carter a patsy.

I yanked open the door of the Rolls and twisted the

key in the ignition. The motor throbbed to life, and I depressed the clutch and pulled the gear-shift lever through its gate into first. The black limousine eased out of its birth, and I pointed the silver lady at the top of its classic radiator shell toward Dragon House.

Darkness had fallen by the time I found myself once again outside the looming iron gates of the great estate. The huge dragons loomed more menacing than ever against the blue-black night sky, and the twin beams of the huge Lucas headlights on the Rolls illuminated a ghostly mist rising like the visible manifestation of a chill fever from the lawn that had seemed so healthy only hours before.

I found a telephone recessed in the gate pillar and announced myself.

At the other end of the line there was a sharp intake of breath. "Welcome," said an aged voice. The Survivor, I assumed.

In a moment, the Cyclops eye of a single headlamp appeared at the crest of the slope beyond the gates, and when it drew closer, I could see a golf cart being driven by one of Takatani's white-clad minions.

Drawing a cruciform key from inside his coverall, he inserted it in one of the pillars supporting the gates. There was a faint whir of machinery, and the reclining dragons began to swing from my path.

Takatani's man remounted his machine, swiveled it around in a spray of gravel, and led the way back up toward the manor house.

It was as though I had been expected for hours. The Survivor, unruffled, bowed at me from the base of the steps. At their summit, Takatani's mountainous bulk

128

waited. He, too, bowed but said nothing until we were seated again in his study, where the steaming bowls of tea were already laid out.

"I had no idea I would see you again so soon," Takatani said.

"Nor I," I told him.

He reached for a box on his desk.

"Cigar?" he said.

"No, thank you."

"I have recently developed a taste for them," he said, reaching into the cedar box.

He drew the cigar out. The wrapper was the dark English market type.

"One thing about London," he said. "It is still a vast repository of the best of Havana cigars.

Takatani reached into a desk drawer and rummaged about.

"You don't have a match, do you?" he said.

"No, I'm afraid not."

His hand darted inside the drawer again.

There was a flash of metal within his huge palm, and his callused thumb spun a tiny wheel, drawing spark from the flint of his lighter.

Like most cigar smokers, he made a project of lighting up. I got a good look at the source of the flame. It was not the first time I had seen a lighter like it. There was no forgetting the insignia or where I had seen it. It carried the same black swastika and rising red sun I had seen on the lighter in the desk at Gunther Roessler's Eastern Island Tapioca Company.

"Most interesting," I said.

Takatani was still pulling on the cigar. "Eh?"

"The lighter," I said.

Only the sharpness of his glance betrayed him, and then perhaps only for a thousandth of a second. I had caught him for once unaware. Then the bland poker player's visage took command again.

He pretended to be seeing the lighter for the first time. "Curious," he said. "Probably a wartime souvenir. All sorts of junk in this desk." He placed the lighter in the drawer and thrust it shut. Then he took a long puff of his Havana.

"News?" he said.

"Most distressing," I told him. "For both of us. My wife has vanished."

Takatani's breath hissed in over his teeth.

"Are you certain?" he said.

"No question about it. Violence was involved. My chauffeur is dead."

Takatani shook his head in sympathy.

"Lamentable," he said. "He was no doubt endeavoring to protect your wife."

"No doubt," I said.

"So it has spread now to Arab women," he said.

"I don't follow you," I said.

"The violence," Takatani said.

I looked at him in innocent puzzlement.

"Perhaps the world of Arab oil traders is not as small as we sometimes think," Takatani said with an indulgent smile. "Violence has attended your colleagues on two occasions recently. One died under rather strange circumstances on a plane not long ago. These things are always surrounded by rumor and hearsay, of course, but word circulated that the poor fellow was killed by a dose of poison gas. Everybody on board assumed he was asleep, but when the plane landed in Los Angeles, there he was—dead.''

"And the second case?"

"Like the first, never solved. A murder, right here in England. London, in fact. Another oil trader. Like the first, he had just completed a deal of some sort. He spent the night carousing. In the morning, his body was found in the courtyard of a slum dwelling. He had been shot. Again, these things are always subject to distortions, especially the way the newspapers report them. But I believe the weapon was recovered. A Luger, if I remember correctly. Shocking, isn't it?''

"Then you think that the same individual or individuals responsible in the other two cases might be responsible for the disappearance of my wife?"

"I think it not unreasonable," Takatani said. "Have you notified the police?"

"I thought it best not to for the time being," I told him. "Perhaps there will be a ransom note, negotiations—the sort of thing that might be jeopardized if the police are involved."

Takatani nodded. "I think you have acted wisely," he said. "But your wife has attracted a good deal of publicity. Her absence will be noticed by the newspapers."

"I've thought of that," I said. "I think it is possible to put them off. Some story about her going off to stay with friends for a few days. The newspapers are easily satisfied."

"Yes, that's true. I think that as regards your wife, you have adopted a proper course. You have my condolences, my sympathies, and my assurance that anything I can do to assist you in this unfortunate matter will be done without hesitation. I am sure that in a short time you will hear from whoever has abducted her. And then, perhaps, the entire matter can be put to rest in a matter satisfactory to yourself and the other parties—whoever they may be."

"I hope you're right."

"But surely," Takatani said, "you have not made a journey of all this distance simply to inform me of your personal misfortune."

"No," I said. "I have come to bring you word from my principals. They are as yet unaware of my personal difficulties."

"You are most discreet and stoic," said Takatani with a slight trace of disappointment.

"I had no wish to burden them at this time," I said. "The possibility that my family problems might have some impact on their decisions as businessmen is abhorrent to me. However, I did press them for an immediate response to you. The sooner my business here is concluded, I thought, the sooner I could devote myself entirely to the problem of my wife."

Takatani bowed his head.

"I salute you," he said. "For you to devote yourself to your business under such distressing circumstances is most honorable."

"I thank you," I said, "although I am afraid that what I have to tell you will distress you."

Takatani sat rigid now in his chair. "Proceed," he said.

"I am afraid that I must inform you that there is no

possibility—absolutely no possibility, now or at any time in the future—of sales to Japan of oil by my principals. As far as they are concerned, as I have told you before, the oil is irrevocably committed."

Takatani's face darkened. There was no need now for him to mask his emotions. He had made clear long before the seriousness with which he regarded his role in obtaining oil for Japan.

"I shall not ask you this time to forgive my anger," he said. "It is the anger of 110 million people."

His eyes glazed over, and his next words were delivered like slow fire from a high-powered rifle. "One hundred ten million people who will not be denied their destiny."

A vein throbbed in his temple. One hand reached out half-consciously and slid open the desk drawer.

I readied myself for an assault.

Takatani's eyes stared off into space, surveying some course of action, some landscape of the future visible only to himself.

As though acting independently, one of his hands rummaged in the desk drawer. When it emerged, it was I who had to fight to control my reaction.

In it was an exact duplicate of Hugo, my stiletto.

With his immense thumb, Takatani tested its steel.

"A fine weapon," I said.

The words broke his reverie.

"Yes," he said. "Extraordinary. Very fine. I like fine things, as you may have noticed. This," he said, turning the weapon over in his hands, "is fine." He placed it gently back in the drawer. "But of no real consequence."

His face darkened again. "I bid you go now," he said, rising from behind his desk. "I made my position clear to you earlier in the day. This is more than business to me. It is a matter of survival. And so I must bid you go. My hospitality is at an end."

I rose and held out my hand.

He shook his head. "The amenities are at an end."

Takatani clapped his hands. The Survivor, who had been waiting outside, swung open the doors to the study, then scurried on his soundless feet to open the main doors.

Takatani strode behind me. As he passed the Survivor, there was a hiss of rapid Japanese. This time, the Survivor made no move to usher me into the car.

So much for hospitality, I thought. *Well, I'm not exactly helpless.* I swung open the door and slid behind the wheel.

Once again, I looked out, my eyes shifting toward the window where I had last seen Fleur. This time it was empty, a sightless eye staring back at me.

I lowered my gaze. The Survivor had vanished.

There was only Sasuke Takatani, standing at the top of the stairway. As I gazed, a shaft of moonlight broke from behind scudding clouds, illuminating his huge figure like monument—but a brooding and malevolent monument. Hatred radiated from him.

So be it, I thought.

I twisted the key in the ignition and felt the Rolls spring to life. I depressed the clutch, shifted into first, and started the final journey of Sheikh Sharif Sultan al-Qadi from Dragon House.

Down below, at the foot of the incline, I saw the huge

iron gates swing open. The Rolls eased through, and I pointed the Flying Lady back toward London.

A mile of country road passed. Two. And then, in the rear-view mirror, I became aware of headlights.

Someone was behind me. And moving fast.

I depressed the accelerator. The big black limousine responded. So did the other car, the huge beams of its headlights cutting through the night mist.

I rolled down the window beside me.

Out there in the damp night, I could hear the whine of superchargers and the roar of an unmuffled exhaust.

I pulled my head back in and depressed the accelerator another notch. On the big speedometer, glowing greenly in the darkness, the needle edged past the ninety mark.

Still the other car gained.

I gazed quickly into the rear-view mirror.

A vagrant shaft of moonlight glanced off a speck of red as the other machine rounded a curve and broke through a patch of fog.

Bright red. Italian racing colors. The color of blood. I was being pursued by a forty-year-old Alfa Romeo.

There was no mystery about who had sent it.

And when I thought about the stiletto in Takatani's hands, there was no mystery about why.

Chapter 13

I rammed the acellerator to the floorboards. The Rolls, though forty years old, was a thoroughbred. With no sign of laboring, the engine responded. The speedometer needle edged past ninety-five. Ninety-six. Ninety-seven. And then it held. There was no more to give. The huge Lucas beams lanced at patches of mist. On either side, great stands of ancient trees hurtled by. Behind me, the Alfa's lights glared closer, and the even blast of its unrestrained exhaust sounded louder and effortless.

The gap closed to 250 yards. In the rear-view mirror, I could see a goggled driver hunched over the wheel and three white-suited companions with him. And then the road twisted and turned again, and they dropped momentarily out of sight as the big Rolls, rear wheels whining slightly against the macadam, took the corner.

The speedometer had dropped to eighty-eight. I floored the accelerator again and watched the needle climb past ninety-five in a matter of seconds.

In instants the twin beams of the Alfa again flared in

the mirror. The gap was down to 150 yards. Whoever was driving knew his job. And the road. He wasted nothing in the corners. After each curve, he picked up ground. The sporty Alfa was better suited to its work than the Rolls limousine, but still, the driver was making the maximum from the advantages at his disposal.

In a matter of minutes the gap had closed to forty yards. Now the twin beams all but filled my mirror, and at the back of the Alfa I could see one of Takatani's minions pounding the sides of the sleek red car like a frenzied jockey putting the whip to his mount.

There was no question who was going to win this race. Big-hearted as it was, the Rolls was no match for the Alfa.

Up ahead, a straight stretch of road ran between a gauntlet of trees. The Alfa swung out. The whine of its superchargers intensified. The gap between the two cars closed. Twenty yards. Ten. And then the blood-colored machine drew alongside. At the wheel, still hunched, I could see my old acquaintance the smirking chauffeur, his eyes glued to the road but that same condescending smile still pasted to his lean face.

Beside him in the front seat, so close that I could have reached out from the driver's seat on the right side of the Rolls and touched him, a wild-eyed Japanese gestured at me with a pistol to pull over.

I shook my head at him.

He leveled the pistol at me.

I ran the Rolls at the Alfa.

My smirking friend jerked the wheel to avoid me. The Alfa's wheels squealed against the macadam. By the time he straightened it out, he had lost ten yards.

But the battle was still unequal. He was even again in seconds. I could hope that a truck would come at him head-on as he sped down the wrong side of the road, but no vehicle had passed in the opposite direction since I had left Dragon House. It seemed a forlorn hope at best.

Up ahead, I could see the straightaway easing into a right-hand curve. The Alfa pulled ahead. Ten yards. Twenty. Thirty. By the time I hit the curve, it was out of sight.

When I saw it again, the Alfa was pulled across the road, blocking my path. There was a decision to be made in split seconds. Hit the Alfa and perhaps kill myself or stop the Rolls and face the consequences.

I took the big limousine into a controlled skid. There was the anguished cry of protesting rubber as I twisted the big wooden steering wheel. The old car slewed around. Given a fraction of a second more, I might have brought her into a 180-degree turn and led Takatani's people on a merry chase back toward Dragon House. But the distance between the cars as I came out of the turn had been too short. The hindquarters of the Rolls smashed into the right front fender of the Alfa. Bumpers locked.

I don't like to see fine old cars abused, but considering the general air of lethal business about Takatani's people, there was something gratifying about the rending of metal and the shattering of glass on the Alfa that accompanied the impact. One of its headlights collapsed into darkness, and in the midst of everything, I could hear the rim rolling away across the road.

I twisted the big silver light switch on the dashboard, extinguishing the twin Lucases, then flung open the door and hurled myself out in a tumbler's rool that brought me into a shallow ditch beside the road.

I was conscious that my pale robes left me a a good target. But the white coveralls favored by Takatani's people evened the odds.

Wilhelmina was already in my hand. As I peered over the top of the ditch, I saw one of Takatani's men approach the driver's side of the Rolls. The automatic pistol in his hand looked like a Colt .45 M1911 A1, but I was willing to bet that if I examined it up close—a pleasure I was determined to avoid while its owner breathed—it would turn out to be a Japanese Nambu 9-mm Parabellum Model 57A. I remembered Takatani telling me how skillful the Japanese were at adapting to technology of the West to their own needs. The Nambu, produced by Shin Chuo Kogyo, K.K. Ltd. would be just one more example.

The Japanese yanked opened the door and poked the muzzle of his pistol inside.

What came out of his mouth sounded like a curse.

He hurled the door shut and swiveled around in a half crouch, his eyes probing the darkness on my side of the road. He was nicely silhouetted against the glare of the one remaining headlight on the Alfa.

His eyes wide, he inched forward, poking his pistol ahead of him more like an antenna than a weapon as he sought the prey that had eluded him once. He had not yet seen me.

My free hand closed over some pebbles. I tossed them down the ditch. The Japanese jerked his pistol around and fired off a round. There were a spurt of muzzle flash, the whine of a ricocheting bullet, and a metallic ping as the slug rebounded from whatever it had hit and plowed into the Alfa.

It took no linguistic expertise to translate the words that came from behind the bloodred car. In any language there were curses, and then what sounded like orders.

The lone Japanese in my line of sight turned back in my direction. Now he no longer crouched. I could not see his face, but I sensed from his posture that his expression had altered. Where before there had been wariness, now there was heedless determination.

He had been humiliated, and now he was bent on atonement. I knew what was next. But there was almost no time to brace myself.

Like a hate-maddened bull, he charged blindly at where he sensed I was hiding. Gone from his hand was the Nambu. In its place, a stiletto. A wild, animal cry erupted from his throat, making the veins and muscles stand out like straining cables close to the point of rupture.

He had taken no more than two steps before I raised part way up from the ditch, leveled my Luger at him, and put a single shot between his eyes. The impact jerked his head back and cut his unearthly scream from his bulging throat. He tossed backward and lay on the macadam, a white lump against the blackness, his deadly knife glittering beside him. From behind the Alfa came a burst of excited babble. The pistol had taken them by surprise.

The silence that followed was intense.

I strained to hear movement but heard none. I strained to see the start of a flanking operation but could see none.

A minute passed. Two. Three. Only my own breath and a faint stirring of leaves in the trees beside the road broke the soundlessness.

Then a voice called from behind the Alfa. "You come out now. We not hurt you."

"I'm afraid that I can't believe you," I called back.

"Oh," said the voice, "you very much mistaken. We just want to talk with you."

"Out of the end of a pistol or the point of a knife, it seems to me."

There was some falsely heartly laughter, aiming at friendliness. It qualified for no Academy Awards.

"No, no," said a voice. "See, I stand up, raise my hands, show you I mean no harm."

I saw a white specter rise from behind the Alfa.

While my eye was drawn to him, I saw a flash of white out of the corner of my eye. Someone had darted on his belly from behind the Alfa and taken cover in the ditch, perhaps thirty feet away.

"If you want to talk," I said, "then talk."

"Oh," said the voice, "this no way to talk. We not see you. You hold gun on us."

"I find it healthier this way," I said.

"That no way to act. Why not be friendly?"

"I'm friendly only to people who are friendly to me," I said. "I don't think your friend with the pistol and knife, lying out there in the road, was very friendly."

"He a hothead," the voice said. "Disobey orders."

Whoever was coming up the ditch at me was good, but he wasn't lucky. I had seen him start from behind the Alfa to begin with. After that, the rest was easy. Because I was expecting him, I could hear him coming.

He was almost perfect. Very quiet. But in my business, almost perfect isn't good enough.

I faced down the ditch to give him the smallest possible target. And when he came into sight, head first around a slight bend, I sent a bullet into his skull.

He was no more than seven feet away. One arm was outstretched. In his lifeless hand, a stiletto glinted.

"I still don't find you very friendly," I called toward the Alfa. Behind the red barricade, someone pulled down on a door handle. I heard the door open, and then there was darkness. The Japanese had switched off the lone headlight.

"Now, Arab," called a voice I had not heard before, "you die."

"Well at least we're being frank about things," I said.

The silence that followed was more menacing than anything that had gone before.

The moon, which had been flitting in and out of the broad clouds all night, had vanished again. Once more I strained against the darkness, eyes and ears alert for the slightest movement. I heard nothing.

Somewhere in the blackness, though, two men were on the move. And if the one who had died in the ditch was any indication, there were well trained. They would betray little or nothing, and judging by what I had already seen of Takatani's people, there was every likelihood that they would be as precise about killing as they were about the care of fine automobiles.

I moved only my eyes, sweeping both sides of the road. To my left was the ditch, backed by trees. Ahead of me, the road and the two interlocked cars, like the legs of the letter *L*. To the right of the cars, beyond the Rolls, the other side of the road, another ditch, more trees.

Somewhere out there, I knew, a pincer was closing.

I concentrated on the area to my left. Whoever was coming around the other way would eventually have to reveal himself by coming out from behind the Rolls or up from the ditch on the other side. There would be an instant or two, no matter what he did, when he would have to break cover. And that, I was determined, would be a fatal instant.

As for the left arc of the pincer, I would have to take a calculated risk. I suspected that whoever was coming along that side would have considered and rejected the ditch route on the basis of its demonstrated 100 percent fatality rate. Chances were he would swing out wide, perhaps even beyond the line of trees, almost circling me.

I decided to move back and cut him off. I had seen no movement, but the sixth sense that had served me so well in the past told me that unlike his predecessors, this new menace had made it out from behind the Alfa without being seen.

I rolled up out of the ditch, scrambling in a crouched run toward the trees, expecting at any instant to encounter a burst of gunfire and the unforgettable insect chirp of a passing bullet—if not worse.

But the Japanese were busy too. There was only the faintest sound of my own feet skimming over the damp grass before I hurled myself down again under the trees and searched the night anew for the approach of death.

The absence of gunfire was curious. For a moment,

while my senses surveyed the darkness, my mind pondered the possibilities. Either Takatani's men, with the exception of the one with the Nambu, were extraordinarily disciplined, shunning anything short of a certain kill, or they had been out of position or too slow witted to capitalize on my brief exposure to a reasonable shot.

The discipline was a real possibility. The lack of position was fairly unlikely. And I ruled out slow wits. I had seen enough of Takatani to believe that he would find that intolerable.

But there was something else. I thought back to the man with that Nambu. What had the yells been that sounded like instructions? Why had he made his final charge with a knife? And the one in the ditch—I remembered seeing the glint of moonlight on his stiletto.

And then I remembered the replica of Hugo in Takatani's immense hands.

The pattern was clear. First the death by gas on the plane. Then the murder in London with the Luger. And finally, a third Arab—me—was to be found dead with another of Nick Carter's weapons. Not only Nick Carter, Killmaster N3, would be smeared. So would AXE. So would the United States. Arab oil interests would not likely take kindly to that sort of thing; they were likely to respond with a few sanctions that would cut off the flow of Arab oil to America. And waiting to catch them on the rebound, to capitalize on anti-Americanism, would be Sasuke Takatani.

It wasn't a bad scheme—except that Takatani could never have anticipated that the third "Arab" he selected for death would turn out to be Nick Carter.

There was a touch of grim humor to it all. In the

darkness, I found myself smiling. But that was before I heard a faint rustling.

I knew now that I had nothing to fear from a pistol. The orders of the night called for my death by stiletto. One more death arranged by Takatani to throw suspicion on Nick Carter.

It was the little advantage that makes the difference. I could ignore the possibility of gunfire. But whoever was coming at me, remembering the two companions who lay with their heads blasted away only a few yards away, would be expecting another bullet as his payment for any carelessness. He would be expecting to fight me at a distance.

I shifted the Luger into my left hand and flicked Hugo from the sleeve of my robe down into the fingers of my right hand. The balanced steel felt cool and soothing against my skin.

I listened again. There was a rhythm to the rustling. I timed it. Two seconds—move. Two seconds—move. He was three trees away, coming down the side of the line of oaks.

That was his second mistake. Reasonable, but probably fatal. He had chosen that side because out there the trees would never be between him and the ditch. He could cover the terrain fairly well by sight. And he would have had me trapped between him and his confederate if I had stayed in the ditch. So pistol or no pistol, they must have figured that with a well-coordinated princer movement, one of them would have a chance in a final charge to plant a knife blade in the sheikh, clean up the mess in the road, and get out.

I slithered to the left of the line of trees, timing my

movements to coincide with his, until I had reached a fresh refuge behind one of the tree trunks. I listened to him make his way down the other side.

When he came out, head turned toward the ditch, I moved in quickly behind him and treated him—with the help of Hugo—to a swift and quiet death. I had no time for remorse. He would have done the same for me. Only a grunt of surprise burst from his throat when the long blade sank into him.

Three down, I told myself. *One to go.* I wasted no time. What was important was to continue the timing of the pincer movement. I wanted whoever was out there to see a pale figure closing in on the ditch, just as he would have expected. By the time he realized that the pale figure was wearing a robe, not a coverall, it would be too late.

I reversed direction, moving as the dead Japanese had moved—at two-second intervals, traversing the damp grass in an arc curving toward the ditch where the sheikh had last been seen.

When the time came, I was rewarded. From just outside the ditch, I could see the outline of a head, staring out from behind the Rolls. I waved my hand. A hand waved back. And then we charged. It took only a moment for him to realize what had happened. But in that moment I had hurdled the ditch and was out on the road.

For once, the smirk was gone from the face of my old friend the chauffeur.

His face showed momentary surprise, then grim determination. In his right hand, he held another of the Hugos that Takatani had had the foresight to provide.

146

Another example of Japanese adaptation of Western technology, I could not help thinking.

The chauffeur hissed at me as he skidded to a halt, the knife—blade upthrust—aimed at my heart.

"Are you going to shoot me, too?" he asked. He brandished the knife and pointed to the blade glittering in the road beside his dead companion. "Or will you fight like a man?"

I ran Hugo out of my sleeve again. "I have my own, thank you."

"And what about the pistol?" he said. "If things go badly for you, Arab, are you going to take out your pistol and shoot me?"

"No need for that," I said. Keeping an eye on him, I backed toward the Alfa and tossed Wilhemina gently inside.

"All even," I said.

The Japanese bowed curtly. When he straightened up again, I noticed that his smirk had returned.

"Very fair of you," he said.

I stood with my back against the Alfa. "Are you ready to begin?" I asked.

The interlocked cars formed two sides of a square. To my right was the ditch where I had taken refuge. And a few feet out from the corner formed by the interlocked cars lay the body of the Japanese who had charged me.

The chauffeur made a quick survey of the terrain.

"Yes," he said. "Let us begin. Let us get this foolishness over with. You will die tonight, Arab. Prepare yourself for that. You are but one man. And I am the Japanese people."

He bowed once again. I bowed in return.

And then he moved out eagerly, the knife held close to his body, ready to dart and kill, like the streaking head of a deadly serpent.

On that deserted road, surrounded by darkness, death, and destruction, we closed like two ghosts in our pale clothing, with only the polished steel of our weapons to light the way.

The chauffeur was good. He drove well. And now it was clear he knew how to handle himself with a knife. He was more than willing to meet me more than half way. I had only to take a couple of steps from the Alfa before we were within striking distance of each other.

He kept the point of his stiletto in constant, minute motion, changing angles continuously, ready to strike at the first sign of carelessness.

It was likely to be a long, even contest, decided by a single mistake.

Above his blade, his mouth remained fixed in that relentless smirk. And then with his left hand, he beckoned me to come out after him.

"As you wish," I said.

He moved slightly to his right, then pedaled backward as I responded to his challenge.

He took three steps backward, then one to his right. His left leg bucked slightly. The smirk vanished.

I leaped forward for the kill.

And then I felt myself flying through darkness before my headed jolted sharply against the road. My wrist snapped against the macadam, and Hugo, clattering mockingly, bounced away into the night.

I had been led into a trap—spilled oil in the road.

I looked up stunned. Wider than ever, the smirk twisted the chauffeur's face.

"As I said, Arab, you will die tonight."

I shook my head, trying to clear away the fog. My limbs seemed heavy and slow. The Japanese lashed out with his foot, striking the side of my head. I felt my eyes beginning to close as the pain exploded inside my skull.

I shook my head again. He moved slightly. There would be another kick, perhaps, and then I would lapse into unconsciousness. In my mind's eye, I could see the aftermath—the Japanese kneeling over my body, picking his spot, raising his knife high and plunging it in. The geyser of blood from a punctured artery. Then the nothingness of death.

Summoning every ounce of strength, I began to raise my hands, to ward off the next kick. It was going to be fruitless. Sitting on the ground, I had no chance to prevail. The next seconds would be fatal.

"Farewell," said the chauffeur.

His smirk had never been wider.

It was still on his face when the shot rang out through the open rear window of the Rolls. The impact of the bullet thrust him forward a couple of steps before he regained his balance.

Looking up, still dazed, I saw the rear door of the old limousine swing open, and Fleur—holding one of the Arisaka rifles—emerged.

I could only sit there, staring at her glassily as she glided out from behind the door, still in her gray gown, like another of the ghostly family that now littered this little battlefield.

She held the rifle loosely in one hand. And as I watched, the chauffeur, reeling drunkenly, his smirk replaced now by an expression of utter bewilderment, forced his body into a turn.

With his back toward me, I could see the dark bloodstain spreading rapidly across his white coveralls. And then his right hand darted up. Before I could cry out, a glittering point of steel hurtled through the darkness and lodged itself to its hilt just beneath Fleur's ribs.

The Arisaka rifle slid out of her hands. The Japanese slumped to his knees, rocked once, twice, and then, as though drawn backward by the powerful sinews of Death itself surrendered convulsively to his fate. His eyes stared up at the black sky and for once, at last, his face was expressionless.

Fleur still stood in the road, unbelieving, her pale face paler than ever. I struggled to pull myself up. Shaking my head, forcing my leaden limbs to respond, I raised myself from the road and staggered toward her. She collapsed in my arms.

I eased her into a reclining position across my knees while I sat with my back against the Rolls. One look at the position of the stiletto told me that she was without hope. For an instant, I thought again of poor Taffy.

There were tears on her cheeks.

"Does it hurt much?" I asked.

"No," she said. "No."

"I'm afraid there isn't much hope," I said.

One of her cool hands—cooler now than ever—reached out and grasped mine. "Don't worry about it," she said. "I'm glad I could help you."

"I am too," I said. "I don't know what might have happened if you hadn't turned up when you did."

"I decided to stow away in your car," she said. "I couldn't bear to be with him any longer, not when I heard about your woman."

"What about her?" I said.

"He has her there, down in the underground area where he keeps the cars. It's not only a garage. There are other rooms there, and weapons, too. If you don't give him the oil, she will die. And they are torturing her to make sure that when you see her, she will beg you to give them the oil."

"Nice people, aren't they?"

"They will stop at nothing. I know that now. I ran away not only because I cannot stand Takatani but also to warn you, when I reached safety, about the woman."

"And the rifle?"

She smiled faintly. "For them, in case they tried to stop me." Her eyes fixed on mine. "And, perhaps, for you."

I smiled down at her. "You needn't have worried," I said. "You were right. Takatani is finished." There was no reason to disclose my identity to her, but I could offer her some reassurance. "Now that I know what he has done to my wife, he is as good as dead."

"Good," Fleur said. "He should have left your woman alone. He deserves to die."

"How many men does he have there?" I asked.

"Perhaps thirty. They are quartered in the underground area. Today, after you left the first time, I spied on one of their meetings. They are a cadre of some sort.

You must be wary of them—they are fighters. And the old man—the one who serves the tea—you must be wary of him, too."

"Yes, I know."

"Promise me you will be careful. If you die, who is to kill Takatani?"

"Don't worry," I said. "The gate—how does it open?"

She shook her head weakly. "I don't know. I never left the grounds by myself before tonight. I'm sorry. I wish I could help more."

"You've helped enough," I said.

I looked down at her gown. The blood had obscured half her dress. Fleur lay unmoving in my arms—motionless, but still breathing.

"I was so happy tonight," she said. "When you drove out through the gates, I thought for certain you would hear my heart pounding with excitement. Leaving that man, leaving my past behind me, going someplace new. A chance to start again, I thought. And now, look at me."

She laughed, but her laughter ended in a cough.

"I want you to know," she said, "that I know you would have helped me. Just as I sensed that Takatani was doomed, I sensed that you were someone who would help me. Perhaps if I had met you years ago, my whole life would have been different. But that's foolishness, isn't it? Perhaps if Dieter hadn't died. Perhaps if I had left the factory then." She shook her head. "There's no changing it now. Not one bit of it. And I'm off on a new journey. And perhaps, if I had

known it didn't hurt, I might have gone years . . .
and years . . . and years ago.''

Her voice grew faint, and her eyes eased shut.
Fleur's life was over. I eased her into the back seat of
the Rolls. One by one I dragged the Japanese into the
front seat. I collected the weapons and stored them
where they would do me the most good. Then I closed
up the Rolls and bounced on its bumpers, until the two
cars were free.

I looked at my handiwork. The chauffeur, his hands
once again at 10 and 2 at the controls of the Rolls, his
companions stuffed in beside him. Fleur, still pale and
beautiful, sat behind them like some great imperious
lady. In the trunk, I remembered, lay the severed
corpse of Minoru.

What a mess for some poor countryside constable.

I yanked open the door of the Alfa and twisted the
key in the ignition. The engine burbled to life. Then I
reached down and touched a switch. The single eye of
its headlight flared angrily. I eased the clutch down and
pulled the gearshift into first, twisting the wheel in the
direction of Dragon House.

A few yards down the road, I stopped the car and
removed my Arab robes, burying them beneath a tangle
of broken branches. Beneath the robes, I was in Western dress. I reached up and tore away the bit of putty
that gave my nose its hawlike appearance, and with the
help of a tiny vial provided by AXE's special-effects
experts, I removed the dark coloring from my face.

The moon had reappeared from behind the clouds. I
gazed at myself in the rear-view mirror.

Satisfied with my work, I switched on the engine again.

The big Alfa surged over the road, heading back to Dragon House.

It was time for Sasuke Takatani to meet Nick Carter.

Chapter 14

I announced my presence by sending what was left of the Alfa hurtling at sixty miles an hour into the wrought-iron gates of Dragon House. There was a satisfactory groaning of aged metal before the hinges gave way and the huge structures, carried by the Alfa, wrenched loose. The Alfa carried them pat way up the incline before its engine died under the strain.

Crouched in the darkness, I didn't have long to wait. I heard the sputter of a golf-cart engine before the latest of Takatani's troops appeared, drew the little machine to a halt, hopped out, and stood contemplating the wreckage, a puzzled expression on his face.

He was still standing that way when I smashed the edge of my hand into the back of his neck. I could feel the vertebrae part. He pitched forward on the gravel, a thin trickle of blood oozing from his nose.

His coveralls were not a good fit, but they would do to get me close to the house without trouble. I hopped into the golf cart and sputtered my way up the drive.

I was thinking how well everything was going when the bullet tore into the front tire. I fought to control the machine and brought it to a halt.

A slim figure was standing just off the driveway, clutching a rifle in his hand. I could see a wisp of beard. There was no need to be told who it was. Didn't he ever sleep?

"Put your hands up, please," said the Survivor.

He hadn't wasted his years. His frisk picked up the Luger and the stiletto without difficulty. It was probably too much to expect that he would find Pierre, and I was glad to know that the little gas bomb was safe in its accustomed place.

"All right," he said, "march to the house." His Arisaka poked me just once in the back to make certain I understood his words.

Takatani was waiting for me in his study, as unruffled as the Survivor. Tea was steaming in small bowls, and Takatani watched with a certain amused glint in his otherwise expressionless eyes as the Survivor laid out my weapons like trophies of the hunt brought in by some faithful hound.

"Sooner or later I knew you would come, Mr. Carter," he said. "I give you credit for that. But you're a bit too late, you know."

I cast a puzzled look at him.

"The last of the murders took place tonight. Not far from here. An Arab sheikh. By tomorrow it will be all over the world—including the fact that he was stabbed to death with a stiletto. The rest of it will leak out to the right people, the kind of people whose business it is to add up all the little odd happenings that go on day in and day out in odd corners of the world. And when they are added up, they produce some interesting repercussions, don't you think?''

"Sometimes they do," I said. "Then again, there are times when they don't."

"Well," said Takatani, leaning forward so that his mountainous bulk added even more substance to his words, "I am compelled to believe that this is one of those occasions when they do."

I could only stare back at him, one poker player to another. Considering the circumstances, there was always the possibility that he was right.

Takatani reached into his desk and took out his reproduction of Hugo.

"Since your body is going to be found alongside of that of an Arab sheikh, Sharif Sultan al-Qadi, on a road a few miles from here," he said, "I feel I owe you some sort of explanation. I suppose in your business you become accustomed to seeing things in terms of black and white. To you, perhaps, I am the epitome of evil. To myself I am not. Nor are you to me. We are both representatives of our countries, doing what we do out of the most commendable of motives, to wit, patriotism. It is regrettable, Mr. Carter, that it should have been necessary for our courses to collide."

He shrugged as though to indicate our mutual helplessness before the workings of destiny. Then he took a sip of tea and beckoned for me to try it too. "Go ahead," he said. "You have my word of honor it is safe. Have you ever drunk Kuan Yin? A fine Chinese oolong. Rarely seen outside of native communities. But it is to tea what fine brandy is to after-dinner liqueurs. Just the thing to accompany our conversation."

I sipped it. He was right.

Takatani took another sip. "Naturally, I might have chosen someone other than yourself. But you are paying the penalty for fame. Who else, Killmaster N3, is so well documented in so many dossiers by so many intelligence communities in the world? Your weapons. The Luger. The stiletto. The little gas bomb."

He smiled. "It seems to have been overlooked," he said.

Takatani turned the Luger on me and held out his hand. "I think I have the advantage," he said. "So no tricks, please."

I reached into my trousers, pulled out Pierre, and rolled it onto his desk. "Most amusing," Takatani said, "although perhaps not to a certain colleague of mine named Gunther Roessler."

It was my turn to betray surprise.

"Oh, yes," Takatani said. "Yes, indeed."

He reached into his desk and took out the cigarette lighter emblazoned with the swastika-rising sun emblem I had seen before at Roessler's plantation.

"No," Takatani said, "it is not a World War II souvenir. This is the emblem of a new alliance, in which the Japanese are the dominant partner. A few of the old Germans, like Herr Roessler, are with us, useful for some of their specialized interests, determined to press on with what was begun in the thirties. For them, for us, the war is not over. Destiny has an inevitability about it. History is sometimes a glacial force. And so, if in one decade or one century destiny is not realized, perhaps in another decade or another century the time will be at hand.

"People like myself and the late Herr Roessler believe in that. It is unfortunate that he died before he could see the dream realized. But like me, he understood the powerful economic tides that are the keys to victory and the ruthlessness with which they must sometimes be mastered. We are of the same philosophic background. Intense nationalism—unwavering, inextinguishable—is the fuel that drives people like us. I myself am the intellectual heir to a Japanese organization known as the League of Blood."

The League of Blood. What an apt name for them—people like Takatani and Roessler, whose bloated dreams blind them to the rights of others and lead them to mass murder and mass destruction. I looked over at Takatani, himself a bloated figure. A true son of the League of Blood. He and his followers trumpeted Japanese rights in the name of patriotism, heedless of the right of others to live, leaving behind everywhere a trail of blood. I thought of Roessler's jungle death camp, the angry hordes in the streets of Djakarta, of poor Taffy and Fleur. Even the two dead Arabs, on the plane and in the courtyard of that London Slum.

And if Takatani's plans came to fruition, there would be others—Americans, this time—homeless, jobless, hungry, perhaps desperate enough to turn on one another. For Takatani, it must have seemed a wonderful prospect for so little effort. A few small murders rippling out in the sea of geopolitics to become a tidal wave of hate to turn Arab against American, because of suspicions about a man named Nick Carter, to bring oil to Japan and assure its future.

I could not bring myself to accept Takatani's

apocalyptic vision of his country's future. It was, he said, an adaptable nation. Whatever the future held, it would adapt and survive. Takatani was blind to this in his megalomaniacal vision of his role in history.

"I follow your plans," I told him. "But the goodwill of the Arabs that you hope to achieve as a result of throwing suspicion on me? How long do you think it will last?

Takatani smiled. "So you are more than simply a killer, are you? There's more in that head of yours than knowing how to use these weapons?"

"I like to think so."

"The Arabs," he said, "are merely of temporary usefulness. When our reserves are sufficient, we shall be able to move against our neighbors in Asia and thus assure our own supplies."

I raised my eyebrows.

"Oh, yes," he said, as though reading my mind. "You think of Japan as a nation that has abandoned militarism." He shook his head. "Not true. Not while I live. These men of mine are the nucleus of the rebirth of its armies. You see them exercising and fixing cars. That is but a trifle. They are steeped in tradition, as well trained for their ultimate roles as leaders of a new Japanese army, navy, and air force as any graduates of your command college in Fort Leavenworth."

I looked at him skeptically.

"Don't underestimate me, Mr. Carter," he said. "You have seen the old man out there. The one who survived for so many years, alone, on an island in the Pacific, after the end of World War II. I retain others like him. He was but an enlisted man. I retain others of considerably more rank and vision who are capable of learning from the mistakes of the past. When Japan, at my signal, goes to battle the next time, you may be assured that it will not fail.

I thought of Takatani in the poker game, backing his cards when he knew he could win. A chill crept over me. It might take him two years, or five, or ten, but he would wait until the day he held the right cards: oil, money, industry, an army. And then he would move.

Unless I could stop him. Now.

I held out my cup for a refill. Takatani's huge hands seized the fine porcelain teapot with surprising gentleness. He watched with affection as the amber liquid, trailing steam, poured into the tiny cup.

Then he filled his own.

"I don't suppose you will believe me, Mr. Carter, but I am truly sorry that I had to embroil you in this matter. I like fine things. The best. In art, automobiles, women, to name a few. And in your business, you are the best. It grieves me to destroy you, but I am afraid that is going to be necessary. If I do not, then you will destroy me—isn't that so?"

Holding my cup, I pretended to contemplate the possible alternatives, and then with a sweeping motion, I hurled the scalding tea in an arc that crossed Takatani's eyes while I simultaneously dashed to the floor the single lamp that illuminated the room.

An enormous bellow of pain erupted from Takatani's cavernous chest. Behind me, I heard the door bang open as the Survivor bolted in.

Racing past the desk, I crossed my arms over my face and leaped at the huge windows that overlooked the rear of the house. The aged wood cracked, as I had hoped it would, and in a spray of glass and splinters, I flew out onto the soft, damp turf.

A I sprinted to my left, I could hear the snick of a rifle bolt followed by the instantaneous blast and the chirp of a passing bullet from the old man's Arisaka. And then, hugging the line of the house and thanking my stars for the dark suit I had worn under my robes, I was out of his sight and angle of fire.

I looked up at the sky. The clouds were still suppressing the moon. There was always the possibility that the moon would break through at the wrong moment, bathing me in silver light while I made my way across that finely tended grass to the line of trees, leaving me a perfect target. But it was a risk I was going to have to take—and take fast.

I began to spring across the open ground. Even as I ran, I could hear the faint ringing of an alarm bell up ahead of me, and there was no doubt what it was. Someone in Dragon House was signaling the cave, to let its deadly inhabitants know that Nick Carter was loose on the grounds.

I didn't like it at all. For these people, probably bored with exercises, this was going to be war in miniature: Japan against the United States. A military expedition in preparation for the future. It was the sort of thing Takatani would like too. He enjoyed it when he held all the cards.

I hit the line of trees and threw myself beneath the nearest tangle of underbrush, waiting while my heart slowed from what I thought was a pounding that could be heard for yards around.

Ahead of me I could hear excited babble at the mouth of the cave.

The little war was beginning.

Chapter 15

I had seconds to move as close as I could to the mouth of the cave. And when I got there, panting against the moist earth where I had thrown myself, I saw them streaming out, still in those unfortunate—for them—white coveralls. But now they had put away their wrenches, their oil cans, their soft polishing cloths. This time they were carrying submachine guns, at port arms.

There were muttered curses as they trotted from the cave, unaware that their quarry lay within inches of them, and fanned out in the darkness. I gave silent thanks that they used no dogs.

When they had passed by, I made my way cautiously down the incline.

Under dimmed lights, the ranks of Takatani's re-markable collection of automobiles receded into the distance in silent, gleaming ranks. A pair of coveralls hanging on a hook, and as I had guessed, I found a couple of spare submachine guns. I appropriated them, as well, along with a couple of five-gallon cans of gasoline.

I made my way deeper into the darkness of the side passageway and donned the coveralls as replacements for the ones the Survivor had made me surrender.

Then, as I straightened up and prepared to sling the submachine gun, I heard the moaning—so soft at first that I couldn't believe I had heard anything at all.

Farther down the corridor, I could see something I hadn't noticed before—a dim patch of light.

Moving silently, leaving behind the cans of gasoline but clutching one of the weapons at the ready, I made my way toward the light. As I grew nearer, I saw that it came from the rectangular pane of a window set into a passageway wall, like the window of an observation room in a hospital. Beyond the window, a door stood partially open. Through this, I realized as I drew closer, the moans were escaping.

Even before I reached the window, I knew what I would see. Reality confirmd my fears. Leila lay strapped to a table. She was nude. And in a single glance, I knew everything that had happened. Takatani had tried to use her—to persuade the sheikh to see things his way. When he had failed, he had given her to his men, starved for sex and starved for sport. Her face was as beautiful as ever, marred only by the thin smear of blood beside her sensuous mouth and the glaze of shock that spoke more than the blood of what had been done to her. The rest of her body—if you could still call it that—I could barely bring myself to look at. If there was any solace, it was that Leila would soon be dead.

I picked the remnants of her clothes from the floor and wiped the blood from her mouth.

"It's me," I said. "Nick."

"I'm sorry," she said. "I haven't been much help at all."

I put a finger to her lips.

"Don't try to talk," I said.

She shook her head violently in disagreement, her black, blood-flecked tresses flaying the heavy subterranean air.

"I thought I could help you," she said, "but I've only made things worse."

"Don't worry about it," I said.

"I walked right into it. I wanted the car, and they told me the chauffeur had asked me to meet him in the garage. And when I got there, it wasn't Minoru at all. It was someone else, and he. . ."

"He's dead now," I said.

A rush of air escaped her throat. It was difficult to determine whether it was a gasp of pain or a sigh of satisfaction.

She closed her eyes, and for a moment I thought perhaps that death had eased her agony. But she was only marshaling her strength.

"They wanted to use me, to persuade you—the sheikh that is—to reconsider."

"I know. Whose idea was this?" I gestured at the room, the table, the atmosphere of lust and blood and brutality.

'Takatani," she said. "He was the first. And then the rest of them."

So beneath the veneer of civilization, the barbarian lived. One more score to settle.

I loosened the straps that restrained Leila. The blood flowed more freely now.

"Do you think you can walk?"

She nodded, gritting her teeth.

"You can still help me," I said.

I draped her in what was left of her clothes and handed her one of the submachine guns before we began the long, halting walk down the corridor and up the ramp to the mouth of the cave. I stopped along the way to pick up the gasoline cans.

When we reached the mouth of the cave, I could see that Leila had only a few minutes. I propped her in a sitting position. As I began to move away, she clutched my arm. "Don't worry," she said, jerking her head toward the submachine gun in her other hand. "I'll hang on for as long as you need me."

I leaned over and kissed her mouth for the last time. "I know you will," I said.

"I'm sorry, Nick." The words emerged slowly, as if over ridges of pain. "Sorry there isn't going to be more."

"So am I," I said.

And then, picking up the gasoline tins, I moved away, first in an arc, then to the edge of the trees.

My scream, delivered in my best Japanese imitation, brought the first dozen of them running, like boys in a game. It was as I had thought. They had plenty of practice but no experience. And now they were about to find out the difference between games and reality. They came into sight almost simultaneously. And Leila cut them down with her submachine gun.

The next dozen came in like fools too, certain the firing meant that I had been killed. There was a short burst of fire from Leila. A couple of answering bursts. And in the melee, I put a match to the trail of gasoline I had left in a semicircle, trapping the Japanese inside. Now, they had Leila in front of them and a wall of fire in back. They had a choice—make for the mouth of the cave, where Leila waited, or come back out through the wall of fire. They were lost either way. Working from behind a tree, I picked them off both ways—some of them as they came screaming out, like human torches, through the flames; others as they stood illuminated by the flames en route to the cave mouth.

And then there was silence, save for the crackling of the flames in the underbrush. And in a moment, baffled by the dampness of the English countryside, the flames, too, subsided.

Not far away, I could see Leila, still sitting just by the entrance of the cave, surrounded by the dead.

I began to crawl toward her.

As I drew closer, I saw that although her head was lolling on her shoulders, her arms had begun to raise the submachine gun she still held.

The effect was grisly and hair-raising. A woman, by all rights dead, moving mechanically, her eyes unseeing. And then I realized what was happening and loosed a burst of fire that ripped through her corpse in a final indignity that sent the figure behind her rising up like some deadly puppet master. Even in his last moments, he was formidable. In his last moments, he let go of the dead Leila and raised the familiar Arisaka. But it was too late.

The Survivor was dead, his long war over at last.

There was no time to contemplate the ironies that had preserved him in the jungle, only to bring him to this fate in an unfamiliar countryside. From the cave I could hear the thunder of a powerful engine. And immediately I realized what had happened. Under cover of all the fire, the black-robed Survivor and Takatani had made their way in close to the cave. And in the brief pause after his troops had been cut down, Takatani had made his way inside and down the incline, while the old man, in his final act of fealty, had covered for him. And now Takatani was making a break for it.

I readied the submachine gun. The car hit the mouth of the cave at about sixty miles an hour, and I stationed myself for a shot through the windshield.

I squeezed the trigger and waited for the cobweb of glass to testify to my accuracy.

There was nothing.

The weapon was empty.

I threw myself to one side as the huge machine roared past, its lights dark, its exhaust blasting in my ears as it broke out of the line of trees and onto the broad grassland.

I knew now what I had to do. Leila was dead. The cadre that was to form the nucleus of Takatani's new Japan of conquest and domination was indeed a league of blood. But not in the way they had imagined. I left Leila where she was, sitting against the mouth of the cave. Her face was still unmarred. There was a line of wounds at her waist, where some Japanese had finished the job he and his comrades had begun, and then another line, higher up, where I had aimed.

I took a moment to look at the Survivor. His teeth were bared, and he looked like some dog that had died snarling in defense of his master. He was misguided, I thought, but not ignoble.

And then I sprinted down the incline into the cave. I knew what I wanted, and it was waiting for me—a Bugatti type 57.

I was going to need everything it could give me to catch Takatani. I knew what he was driving— a Mercedes-Benz SSK, one of the most powerful automobiles ever built, a brute of a car that only a man with Takatani's strength could hope to control for long.

The car I wanted was the creation of an automotive genius—the legendary Ettore Bugatti, the man they called the Master of Molsheim. And this was going to be a race that would have appealed to him.

I hoped only that the Japanese mechanics had restored it in the way he could have wanted. Ettore Bugatti was a perfectionist.

I worked the ignition, and the engine rumbled to life. I eased the pale blue car—French racing colors—out of the ranks and up the incline. Everything seemed to be working smoothly. I took the Bugatti slowly across the lawn, and when I hit the gravel roadway leading off the grounds of Dragon House, I switched on the lights, hit the accelerator, and began taking the car up through the gears, with the needle on the tachometer hovering at the red line and the speedometer climbing steadily into three figures.

Once again I was on the road toward London, this time the chaser rather than the chased. And somewhere out ahead of me, in one of the most formidable automobiles ever built, a mountain of a man—impelled by a concept of destiny that was heedless of the lives of others—was speeding through the night.

I pressed the accelerator till it touched the floorboards, and the engine responded with no indication of strain. On a brief straight, my eyes swept over the dials. Gasoline tank topped out. Oil pressure normal. Water temperature normal. Engine revs and speed all that could be expected.

There was nothing left to do but steer, shift gears, and brake—and with a Bugatti, there was not much sense in braking.

Like the Mercedes, this was an open car. The wind whistled by, and my eyes scanned the road ahead for the first indication that I was closing the gap on Takatani. Darkness was my answer.

Once again, the twin beams of my headlights bored into the darkness, banishing it as the Bugatti raced through the damp night. Beside me there was the rush of wind and the long rows of trees flanking the roadside. Familiar terrain, including a stretch where skid marks showed where I had turned the old Rolls around to slew it into the Alfa. The huge black car was still sitting there, and a second set of skid marks in the road showed that Takatani had managed to avoid it.

I smiled grimly. At the speed he was traveling, he could barely have had time to more than recognize the car. And its presence there must have given him some joy at the thought that the sheikh was dead. And even if Carter were alive, the basic plan was operative. For the world at large, another murder to be charged to N3.

Anger flowed through me. I pressed harder on the accelerator. But it was already rammed against the firewall.

The road swung in a wide arc, and up ahead, perhaps a mile or so, I saw headlights flashing between the columns of trees. They were moving fast. Takatani. I figured that I had cut the margin between us in half since I had first started out.

I was managing to keep the Bugatti at top speed, but there was no way I could coax more out of its engine. In my mind's eye, I could see again the Alfa as it pursued me down the road, with one of Takatani's men pounding its sides like a jockey urging on his mount. I felt a temptation to do the same. But though the Bugatti was a thoroughbred, I knew it could give no more.

It was going to come down to a question of driving skill, of picking up inches and feet in the corners, a split second here, a split second there, until the gap closed and I could draw even with Takatani, force him from his car or off the road, and finish his dream of conquest and death.

Or so I hoped.

There is more to a road race than drivers and machines. There are mechanics as well. And there are those who will tell you that mechanics are the people who really win races.

At first I thought it was a wisp of ground fog floating across the horse-shoe-shaped radiator shell. And then I realized it was a wisp of steam.

A quick glance at the water-temperature gauge confirmed my fears. I eased back on the accelerator, shifted into neutral, and let the car coast for a few seconds. If there was any cooling, it was imperceptible on the gauge.

I shut off the engine and waited by the side of the road while the second hand on my watch made one complete revolution. The steam had vanished, but when I switched on the engine again, I knew that for all practical purposes the race was over.

There was no chance now of overtaking Takatani. The battle now was simply not to lose him. Every minute I remained idle at the side of the road was costing me at least a mile and a half, perhaps more. I switched on the Bugatti's engine once more and eased out onto the road. At sixty miles an hour, the engine seemed disinclined to overheat. So be it, I thought. At least I would fall back only half a mile or so a minute.

After the frenzied pace earlier, sixty miles an hour seemed like crawling. There was time to notice that night was giving way to day, the sky graying and the trees shedding their blackness. Here and there, a light showed in a house, and finally a man appeared, walking beside the road.

I brought the Bugatti to a screeching halt.

"Have you seen a big open car come by?" I asked.

"Aye," he said. "Going hell bent." He pointed down the road.

"Many thanks," I said.

Takatani wasn't going to be hard to follow. A Mercedes Benz SSK is not an inconspicuous car. And Takatani was not an inconspicuous man.

Which was how we all wound up at Heathrow Airport with all hell breaking loose.

Chapter 16

The place was electric with tension. All I had to do was let my instincts guide me along the line of highest voltage. And there, off in a corner of a lounge, cut off from the public by a squad of burly London constables, I saw the little knot of VIPs I had expected to see.

One of them was very familiar.

"All right," he snarled. "Let him through, Constable. I'll vouch for him."

The big policeman, still staring skeptically down on me, jerked his head in the direction of the VIPs, and I strode past him and stuck out my hand to Hawk.

"Forget the amenities," he said. His cigar was clenched between his teeth, its tip an angry red as he pulled on it.

"I never expected to see you here," I said.

"I wouldn't be here except for you," he said. "Getting yourself captured. Having to ransom you from the Israelis. Having to hang around here like a mother hen as part of the bargain. And now this."

"Now what?" I said.

"He's yours, isn't he?"

"Who?" I said with less than complete candor.

"The Japanese, the one out there."

He waved his arm toward one of the windows overlooking the sprawling airfield.

"Out where?"

"Dammit!" Hawk said. He grabbed my arm, digging his powerful, stubby fingers into my biceps like some irascible schoolmaster, and led me to a window.

"There's a Japan Air Lines 747 out there," he said. "And your friend's aboard it."

"So?" I said. I was beginning to enjoy his rage in some crazy way that eased the fatigue and tension of the preceding twenty-four hours. "He has a ticket, doesn't he?"

"Very funny," said Hawk. "Very funny. You know damn well what he's done." He looked up at me, and the anger faded from his face. "Or do you?"

There was something in the way he looked at me that made me realize that the time for teasing was over.

"He's taken over the plane, hasn't he?" I said.

"That's the least of it," Hawk said, lowering his voice. He jabbed a thumb toward the animated knot of VIPs.

"You know what we've got there?" He said. "Home office. Foreign Office. British Intelligence. London Police. All on the highest level, to say nothing of our Israeli friends. And do you know why? Not just because your Japanese friend climbed onto an airplane. The airplane is empty. They could blow him out of the damn thing in a minute if they wanted to. In fact, they sent a little punitive expedition out there when he first boarded the plane. He stopped them with a little note he dropped out of the cockpit.

"What did it say?"

"It said that unless they had a crew aboard in an hour and permitted the plane to take off without interference for a destination he would name, bombs would be set off."

I shrugged.

"You think it's routine only because you haven't heard the beauty part yet," Hawk said. "Up to the note, it was fairly cut and dried. Local police, airport security, and all that. After the note is when the phones started ringing, when the Home Office, the Foreign Office, and my old friends from British Intelligence got into it—the kind of old friends who knew I was in the area and asked if I might know anything about the Japanese on the plane and word that had just come in about a car full of dead Japanese on a country road and some sort of massacre of Japanese on a country road and some sort of massacre of Japanese on an estate in Oxfordshire.

"Now, you must remember that some of these friends and I go back a long way together, and so I told them that it might just be possible, although I wasn't certain. And so they . . ." Hawk paused. "Invited me—yes, that's the word—invited me to come out here to the airport with them and give them the benefit of my thinking on this matter. And then, of course, you— you, Nicholas—showed up, and any doubts I might have had about all those Japanese were dispelled."

Hawk fixed me with an angry gaze.

"Well, you're right," I said. "But all those others

don't add up to much—at least, they don't any more. That one on the plane, though—he's big trouble. What was in the note he sent out?''

"Bomb threats are a dime a dozen, aren't they?" said Hawk. He didn't wait for me to answer. "Not this one. You see, your friend out there—"

"Takatani is his name—Sasuke Takatani."

"Says they're planted in certain schools. Now these aren't just any schools. These are the sort of schools where the English aristocracy send their sons. And not just the aristocracy. Royalty. Let's not forget royalty. We're in jolly old England now. So if there are any slipups out here, or anywhere else, it isn't going to be just a one-day sensation. Killing kids is bad enough. But there are some people I know in this business who would tolerate it, as long as it isn't their kids. This time it just might be their kids, so those people over there"—he jerked his head at the VIPs—"aren't likely to be in a state to make a cool decision.

"The Israelis say they ought to blow your friend out of there anyway—you can't give in to people like Takatani. They say there's probably enough time to evacuate all the schools before a little expedition goes out and deals with your friend. The British say they can't take the chance that someone doesn't get the word in time—and they don't know which schools are involved anyway."

"He's bluffing," I said.

"Talk is cheap," Hawk said.

"He's bluffing," I repeated.

"And if you're wrong?"

"I'm not wrong."

"Look, Nicholas," Hawk said, "why don't we leave this to the British? It's their country and their kids."

"If he gets away, it's our country and our kids. I haven't got time to explain everything, but you have to trust me on that."

"All right," he said. "I'll take that on faith. But the bluffing business is something else again."

"Let me see if I can convince you." I told Hawk the story of that night of poker at Madlock's—that night when Takatani had backed only winning cards up to the very end, when he had resorted to a colossal bluff. "And now he's bluffing again," I said.

"I still say you could be wrong," Hawk said.

"I'm not," I told him. "But even if I am, we still can't let him get away. He has got to be stopped. Here. Now."

I guess there was something in the way I said it that made Hawk realize that not just a few—but perhaps millions—of lives were at stake.

"All right," he said. "I hope you're right. If you're not . . ." His voice trailed off. "I'd rather not think about it. What do you propose?"

"Is there anyone from Special Effects around?"

Hawk smiled one of his Machiavellian smiles.

"I had time to make a phone call before I went to meet my British friends, and I think, Nicholas, that if we go for a little stroll, we might just bump into someone from Special Effects."

Hawk was still smiling when he said, "Coming through, Officer," and one of the burly constables stepped aside to let us pass out into the thronged corridors of Heathrow. The VIPs, still huddled, were unaware of our departure.

There was a big Rolls waiting outside. Nick Carter entered. Five minutes later, Sheikh Sharif Sultan al-Qadi emerged, flowing robes, dark sunglasses, and all.

Two minutes later, accompanied by a small, cigar-smoking man packing an impressive set of credentials identifying him as a very distinguished official from the Home Office, the Sheikh had passed through the last airport security checkpoint and was making his way alone across the tarmac to the looming JAL 747.

I could see movement up ahead of me in the cockpit.

"Hello," I called. I swept the sunglasses dramatically away from my eyes and waved at the plane. "It is I—Sheikh Sharif Sultan al-Qadi. We must talk."

Takatani's voice floated down. "No," he said.

"Not even of oil?" I asked.

"Do you take me for a fool?"

"Do you think you can afford *not* to speak with me of oil?"

"This is a trap," he said. "You are working with the British."

"No," I said. "It is business. My oil was committed to British interests. In view of your activities this morning, they say they are willing to release my principals from their commitments and to cede their oil to you in return for your word that no harm will come to the schools. They have children in those schools."

"How can I be certain that this is true?"

"You have my word, but I do not ask you to take my word. I have here the appropriate documents, which need only to be signed by you." I reached into my robes and brandished a sheaf of papers.

"How can I be sure that you do not lie?"

"On the basis of our past conversations," I said, "it is a risk you must take, is it not?"

There was a long silence from the poker player aboard the plane.

And then Takatani called out, "Come aboard."

Chapter 17

He was waiting for me just outside the cockpit door, seeming larger than ever in the confines of the plane. He still wore his black robes, and in his sash, I noticed a short samurai sword. One huge hand rested on its ornate hilt.

"I did not believe we would meet again," he said.

I said nothing then of his efforts to kill the sheikh.

"It was destined," I told him in my best Arab style.

"Do you truly have oil for me?"

"As truly as you will kill those children if I do not," I said.

His hand tightened on the sword hilt.

"Do you know what will happen if you lie?" he said.

"Yes," I said. "Yes, indeed. And that is why I decided to lend my services to the British as an intermediary. You must understand their concern for the fate of their children. I said to them: 'Mr. Takatani is a man who is most serious about protecting the future of his country. And most determined to assure its future through the acquisition of oil. And most angry at anyone who stands in his way.' Of course, there was some tendency to doubt me. But then I told them that you were so angry when I was unable to sell you my oil because it had been promised to the British that you actually tried to have me killed.''

"I am afraid there has been some sort of misunderstanding,'' Takatani said.

"No, I think not,'' I told him. "However, no harm came to me, and so I will be forbearing. I understand, my friend, the intense passions business can arouse. Let bygones be bygones. I assure you I am here strictly on a humanitarian mission. I volunteered my services strictly in the name of humanity.''

"You are a strange man,'' he said.

"You also,'' I said.

"What sort of arrangements have you made, and how do I know the commitments made here today will be honored?''

"The oil. Free passage. As for honoring the commitments, I seem to recall that you are something of a gambler. Again I say I think you must run the risk. Should the British renege on the oil, you are no worse off with regard to it than you are now, but at least by then you will be far away. But possibly they will not renege—for fear of your future vengeance, perhaps. Or because they are a sporting people, and if you best them in this matter, they will abide by the result and honor their commitments. As between you and me, I think you should leave them with the impression that if they fail to keep their word vis a vis the oil, they can expect their schools to be bombed at some time in the future.''

Takatani smiled. "I thank you for your counsel,'' he said.

"And,'' I said, "since my principals will be the

shippers, I think you may count on us to see to it that you get the oil, regardless of what the British want. After all, the British cannot afford to have us be insulted by using me as an intermediary and then refusing to honor their bargain. So rest assured, the oil is yours."

Takatani smiled. "Splendid. A most remarkable turn of events."

"Yes, Almost too good to be true."

"Yes," he said. "I feel the same way."

I reached up as though to salute him, and stripped the knob of putty from my nose. Takatani blinked.

And then I shucked of the robes and pulled out the Luger. "Don't move," I said. With my free hand, using a saturated cloth provided by Special Effects, I wiped away the makeup.

Takatani gasped. "Carter!" he said.

"The sheikh is dead," I told him. "Only I put him to rest, not you."

Takatani had recovered his composure. "Go back to your people, Carter. Tell the British their children will die in less than ten minutes unless this plane takes off."

"No," I said. "I'm going to stand here for the next ten minutes, I think, and enjoy watching you. I'm calling your bluff."

"Bluff," he said. "Do you think I'd bluff about something like this?"

"As a matter of fact, yes," I said. "Definitely yes."

"You underestimate my power. You're a fool, Carter.

"Well, I'm willing to wait for ten minutes to find out."

He stood there staring at me. And I stared back. Two

players across a card table, with life and death as the stakes. There was utter silence aboard the plane. The airport, I noticed, was absolutely still. Usually a hive of screaming jets, it was now soundless. All traffic had been halted.

Takatani suddenly pivoted.

"Hold it!" I said.

He fell to his knees, his back toward me. I saw his huge arms move, and then I saw him raise the gleaming blade of his samurai sword. He acted before I could restrain him, plunging the razor-sharp blade slowly into his abdomen and drawing it across in the ritual of suicide known as *seppuku*.

I came up behind him. He sensed my close presence.

"I have failed," he said softly. "I must die. Please help. It is the custom. Shoot me please, lest I betray my pain."

"No trouble at all," I said. I thought of the dead, especially of Leila, especially of Taffy.

I pressed the muzzle of the Luger to the back of Takatani's skull and squeezed the trigger.

The action was smooth—a tribute to abundant oil.